Secrets of Trillium Falls

Mary Vine

Windtree
Press

Secrets of Trillium Falls

Published by Windtree Press in cooperation with Melland Publishing, LLC.

Windtree Press

https://windtreepress.com

Melland Publishing

Caldwell, ID 83607

https://mellandpublishing.com

ISBN Ebook: 978-1-950387-16-8

ISBN Print: 978-1-950387-19-9

Publishing History 1st Edition 2013, A Haunting in Trillium Falls. Published by Wild Rose Press (Wildflower Edition)

2nd Edition 2021 Windtree Press

eBook ISBN: 978-1-950387-16-8

Print ISBN: 978-1-950387-19-9

Published in the United States of America

CHAPTER 1

"*H*ave you lost your senses?" Grandpa tried to raise his weak voice as Taylor helped him out of the car. "Did you hear me?"

"Yes, Grandpa." She didn't know whether to laugh or cry, but at least she'd worked up his dander, which she hadn't done in a good year. Not since her grandmother's death and the deep depression that followed.

"It looks haunted," he half said, and half grumbled.

"It won't when it gets a nice coat of paint."

Taylor watched him look at the house through all three levels of his trifocals. "Looks like an awful big house to paint. I imagine it will cost a pretty penny, not to mention the roof. The roof needs replacing. Probably should have been replaced ten years ago."

She patted his shoulder. "That's the first two things on the list, Grandpa, everything else can wait. I have a break coming up and that'll give me a chunk of time to start fixing things."

Taylor truly was ready to do just that, preparing for the coming move by reading about restoration and taking as many workshops as she could fit into her schedule.

"So you can wallpaper, huh?" He raised his voice again. "That's all you know how to do."

That's all he'd seen her do, but a healthy, able-bodied woman like herself could do a lot to get this place in order. One day he'd be eating his words, but not today. She tried to draw his attention away from the roof. "Look over there; someone put in rose bushes."

"Humph."

She rubbed the back of her neck. "Let's go inside."

They walked over rickety steps and loose floorboards on the porch. Taylor used her shoulder to push the sticking door open.

"Nice hardwood floor, that's one thing I can say for the place," Grandpa said, stepping into the foyer.

Taylor smiled, encouraged. His doctor told her that he needed to get involved in life again. He used to restore homes on his summer breaks from teaching school. It gave him great joy as well as a retirement fund. She hoped her interest in restoring this house could spring him back into action.

"It's an arts and crafts house, see? Look at the moldings. And I love the diagonal pattern on the edge of the hardwood floors. The realtor said these are tongue and grove mahogany floors. This house has lots of potential and will be nothing short of grand when we get through with it."

Grandpa slowly moved himself along the wall with a hand until he reached an adjoining room. Taylor watched him study the cracked ceiling and walls.

"One, two, three, four, five layers of wallpaper. Well, here's the start of your wallpapering job," he said with a smirk.

"As you well know, when you work for the school system, you have lots of days off, so I'll have plenty of time to do it," she said with a forced smile. "It's nice to cut way down on my driving time to work now that we live closer. It's been a long drive for the last two months."

"Humph."

"The heat and the plumbing are intact. We can live through all the rest until you get your energy back. Won't it be fun for the two of us to work on this together?"

He leaned back against the wall; his breathing labored. Lines of exhaustion showed on his face. Sounding defeated, he said, "What have I agreed to sign for? Is this the house I'm going to die in?"

Her heart plummeted and she felt a twinge of guilt for persuading Grandpa to sign for the house sight unseen. "No, Grandpa. This is the house you're going to *live* in."

She looked back into the living room. The gloomy dark shadows gave her an eerie feeling. She shivered. The wind blew and she heard a shutter, or maybe a piece of loose siding, banging against the house.

Getting Grandpa back to the car wasn't easy; he'd used up all his strength complaining about the mess they were in. Her positive outlook took a nosedive as well.

After she ushered him out and to the car, a late model black pickup pulled alongside them in the driveway. Taylor watched a man with tawny, nearly shoulder length hair open the door and step out.

Once Grandpa was settled, she shut the door.

"Hello," he said, sticking a hand out in greeting. He gave a crooked smile, exposing even white teeth. She had to drag her gaze away from his mouth as he continued speaking. "I'm Dillon Nash, the former owner. I'm looking for Taylor Glenn."

"I'm Taylor Glenn. How can I help you?"

"I wanted to show you, or perhaps your husband, a few things about the house. Like where the water main is, for example."

"Sure, you can show me."

"I'll wait for your husband." He stretched his neck trying to look around her into the car.

"No, that's not necessary."

He straightened. "No offense but I'd prefer to show him."

Albeit she was five-foot-two and small boned, yet far from being helpless. "I'm not married. But that shouldn't matter to you."

"It's not that I'm stereotyping, it's just that this house needs a strong back."

Taylor stroked her throat with a hand and grimaced at him, then turned to see Grandpa dosing off, hardly a surprise as he spent most of his time hibernating these days. Further, she believed he pulled away from life by escaping into sleep.

She turned back to Dillon and crossed her arms. "I have a minute now. Please, show me."

A frown below golden-brown eyes, fringed with long eyelashes, ruined his handsome face. "Wait, I thought I saw two signatures on the paperwork."

"You did. Grandpa, here." With her thumb she pointed toward the car window. "The other signature was mine, of course."

"Excuse me for asking, but who will be doing the repairs?"

She could understand his concern since he carried the contract on the house. "My grandfather Gilby, and I."

Dillon looked over at Grandpa and then back again. "Have you ever renovated a house, Taylor?"

"I'm a teacher by degree, but Grandpa has lots of experience and I've helped him in the past." She was not about to explain Grandpa's illness, besides, why should it matter to him anyway? He would get his money. She pointed toward the house and smiled. "Can you show me the water main?"

His eyebrows furrowed. "Is there a boyfriend or someone else who can help you?"

The changes in her life proved difficult and she certainly did not need someone to tell her she couldn't handle her problems. Taylor wanted to tell him that women did more than birthing babies and cleaning house these days. Instead, she sighed in frustration and then forced herself to be pleasant, despite her instincts. "No," she said evenly, "just my grandfather and me."

He sighed in return before turning toward the house. "All right, come this way." She followed close enough to notice how his black t-shirt, tucked into worn blue jeans, fit his broad shoulders. He was a big, healthy, attractive male. Simply being in his presence made her long for a relationship with a man, reminding her what she'd missed over the last year. Yet, she didn't need another man to tell her she needed to branch out on her own and leave her grandfather for someone else to tend to.

He led her to the basement from an outside door. She'd hoped to avoid this section of the house for quite a while, fearing a multitude of spiders. But she had no intention of acting all girlie around this macho man. She could endure the spiders if she had to.

Entering, she used her hands and arms to partially cover her face and hair and went down the six steps.

The air felt cool and smelled musty. The ceiling topped out at about seven feet, with exposed wiring and pipes of various sizes trailing along the floor joists above her. She doubted she'd ever seen so many spider webs in one place before.

Dillon walked over to the far corner, past an old workbench and turned to her. "What's the matter, did you bump your head?"

She smoothed out her long blonde hair with the palms of her hands and then put her arms to her sides. After a nervous chuckle, she said, "No, I didn't want the spider webs to get in my hair."

He frowned but said nothing, then turned, bent down, and tried to twist the handle.

"I'd forgotten that it's partially broken. Would you hand me the vise grips over on the bench?"

After glancing around for spiders, she put an arm up to her head and then down, trying to hide her fear from him. She stepped the few feet to the workbench. About five or six tarnished and corroded tools lay before her on the workbench. She could see why he left them behind. Taylor had taken enough courses to learn several tools but was unsure about a vise grip.

Diving in anyway, she picked up a tool with her index finger and thumb and turned toward him. Next time she'd have to carry gloves and a mask, she decided.

"No, that's a wrench. They are similar, but the grips can be locked into position."

Of course, she knew that was a wrench, but she didn't see what else he'd possibly use on the water main. After carefully laying down the wrench so she wouldn't stir up the dust, Taylor swatted at her chest, hoping she smashed a spider that she just knew went down her shirt.

He shook his head and came to stand beside her.

She got a whiff of lime aftershave when he reached across to grab the right tool. A rush of goose bumps raced through her, and she swallowed against the sensation. An irrational desire made her wonder what it would be like to kiss that strong jaw and be as close to him as his own skin. Quickly, she closed her eyes in the event he might be able to decipher her thoughts.

"Now, remember this tool, because you may have to use this to shut off the water."

"Of course, but that's the a... The mole wrench."

"That's another name for it, yes." Dillon made sure the valve turned with the vise grips and then reached out to take Taylor's wrist. Hand over hand he moved the vise grips back and forth so that Taylor could get the feel of it.

She also got the feel of the calluses on his palm rubbing against her knuckles and enjoyed the sensuousness of having a big male hand fit over her small one. She lifted a finger to her cheek to wipe away a strand of hair and the light scent of his aftershave had transferred from his skin to hers.

"There, that should do it," he said and stepped away from her.

Taylor followed him into the house to view the crawl spaces and fuse box.

Outside, Dillon pointed to the shed. "When I bought the house, I found that someone had left some boxes, tools and equipment in the shed that I thought the next owner might want. I can haul them away if you prefer."

"I'd like to go through them. Thank you."

He pulled keys from his pocket. "I noticed the other day that I have an extra key on my ring that belongs to Calvin's apartment. Here you go."

Taking the key, she said, "Calvin's apartment. I don't know what you mean."

For a moment he looked at her, saying nothing. "Certainly, your realtor told you about Calvin Sweeney, right?"

"No."

"*What?* I can't believe your realtor didn't tell you. It can't be legal. You have a boarder in the apartment that joins in the back. He's a harmless old man that's lived there for the past five years. He lives here rent free in exchange for grounds upkeep."

Not something else, she thought to herself. She felt the now familiar pang of fear in her chest, reminding her that due to Power of Attorney, she was a twenty-three-year-old making decisions for a man in his seventies. She wondered if adding more stress to what she already inflicted on Grandpa might push him over the edge. As it was, he hadn't an ounce of energy and he slept most of the time.

She took a visual sweep of the grounds. Only the front yard had been tended, the rest was a mass of weeds and bushes. Calvin probably had little more energy than Grandpa. "But I already have a harmless old man to take care of."

"Then let him go. It's as simple as that."

Yes, as simple as that. For him, maybe. However, for her, putting someone out on the street was another matter. She put a hand to the back of her neck and sighed.

Dillon gently touched her shoulder. "Do you think you've made a mistake buying this house?" he asked softly. "It carries a lot of baggage and as much as I want to sell it, I believe that you have grounds to pull out. If you'd like to pull out, I understand."

Grandpa's survival depended on giving him something to rebuild. This was the only house in Trillium Falls that fit the bill.

"I appreciate the offer, but I want this house. And thanks for stopping by." She walked back toward the house then turned to say, "And don't worry about me. I promise you, if I have a problem with the water, I'll be able to turn it off with that... thingy."

Dillon gave Gilby Glenn one more perusal before getting into his truck. He guessed the man to be in his seventies and judging by the pallor of his skin and the way he dozed midday, he'd bet his business that Gilby was a sick man.

As he put his keys into the ignition, his eyes followed the sway of Taylor's perfect hips around the bend of the house on her way to meet Calvin. Judging by the fairness of her skin, the blonde hair was no doubt natural. Taylor's facial features were pronounced; her large green eyes matched her full lips. He loved the look of her.

He wondered if she'd ask Calvin to leave or stay. Not his business, he decided. What he really wanted to do was scoop up this woman and take care of her something awful. In more ways than one.

Dillon smiled as he remembered the way she fought to keep real or imaginary spiders away and picked up a tool with two fingers to keep her hands clean. Taylor had to be the prissiest woman he'd ever seen. Albeit the most entertaining.

No way could this prissy woman take on this house. No way was this man, Gilby, going to rise and bring a three-story Victorian house to completion.

He already knew it would cost an arm and a leg to pay for a

professional renovation. He doubted they were rolling in dough with Gilby retired and Taylor making a living as a teacher. If they were, Taylor wouldn't be driving a ten-year-old car. Yet, with or without money, they're going to have a heap of trouble finding suitable help.

What possessed the woman to buy this house? It didn't make sense. Damned if he wasn't going to find out.

CHAPTER 2

*G*randpa was still asleep, so she headed to the back of the house to inspect Calvin's apartment. She nearly ran into him as she cleared the corner.

The man stood no more than five-foot-six, with protruding belly and disheveled clothes.

"You must be Calvin. I'm Taylor Glenn," she said and stuck out her hand.

"Yes, I'm Calvin. I was expecting to see you one of these days as the sign says sold and all."

"Yes, I'm sorry no one has given you any information. I just heard about you today."

"Oh, that's not good. I suppose you're going to want me to move out then, huh?"

He looked so sad. Why did she have such a soft spot for old men? It was his home after all. She really didn't know what to do. "Don't go jumping to conclusions just yet, but I'd like to see the living quarters."

Calvin took off his cap and rubbed his salt and pepper crew

cut. "Oh, of course, Miss. I suppose your husband will want to see it, too."

"No, it's just my grandfather and me."

"Grandfather, huh? Guess I'll have someone to play chess with," he said with a smile.

Taylor liked this idea because she'd moved her grandfather from his home and friends. Due to his illness, he couldn't live alone. She didn't want to take him so far away, yet teaching jobs were scarce in their hometown of Boise, so she accepted her first teaching job in the small town of Trillium Falls.

Calvin escorted her into the small apartment. "This section of the house was once the maid's quarters."

Although his apartment was in much better condition than the main house it possessed no frills, everything appeared stark and drab. A few posters hung on the walls as well as some old, framed prints with snapshots stuck in them. The carpet was dirty from a lack of vacuuming, and the sofa heavily worn in places. If the dishes were clean on the counter, they needed to be put away.

"You hardly have room to turn around in here."

"Oh, but its home. I like it here. Pardon the mess, but it's the gardening I love and spend my energy on." When Taylor didn't answer, he added, "The backyard... Uh, I was waiting for the new owners to tell me what to do with it."

Taylor rubbed her chin. Even if she wanted him to leave, she doubted he could afford to move. How could she cast him out into the street? She couldn't. Besides, she really thought that he could be a friend for Grandpa. Still, she hoped she wasn't making a mistake. "You can continue to stay. We'll see how it goes, Calvin."

He grinned. "Thank you, Miss! I'll do a good job with the yard now that you're here.

Taylor nodded then walked the sidewalk leading to the front of the house.

A wave of melancholy stirred within her. Every so often she

longed for the normal life of someone her age, with the freedom to go out at any time, have a date, or share interests with friends. At times, she felt like a confined child looking longingly out a window at the other children playing. It seemed like a lifetime ago that her life was normal. Actually, it was a year ago when her grandmother was alive, and Grandpa was well.

Just as quickly, the sad thoughts fled, and she felt ashamed of her momentary lapse into self-pity. After all, things had been falling into place, and now her grandfather will have a new friend.

Later at home, Taylor's imagination ran wild because of the eerie noises she'd heard when she took Grandpa through the house. She remembered the family doctor's advice about how pets helped the elderly. She wasn't going to live in that big house without a dog. After deciding she wanted a large dog and a smart one, she checked the Sunday newspaper for German Shepherds. She ran her finger down the column. "Puppies, puppies, puppies," she read.

"Tell me you're just trying to wake me up." From his perch on the couch, Grandpa looked at her with concern and certainly not for the first time since he viewed the house. "You're not thinking about getting a puppy, are you?"

She hadn't realized she'd spoken aloud. He would have to find out eventually and frankly, she was tired of not sharing everything with him in lieu of stressing him out. "Don't you think having a pet would be nice? After all I'm at work all day."

He sat up taller. "You know as well as I do that I can't be running after a puppy all day. Where is your logic these days?"

"All right, then we won't get a puppy."

He visibly exhaled.

"We'll get a dog. I'll try to find a German Shepherd. Maybe one that's older."

"Why such a big dog? You know it will sound like a horse running on wood floors in that big house."

"And it might keep you awake?" she asked with a teasing tone of voice, then turned serious and said, "I would feel more comfortable…in the house if we had a dog."

"Yes, it's a scary old house. You should have taken me through the house before we signed the papers. You were in such a damn hurry." He lay back down and turned his face to the couch.

Her childhood thinking flooded back to her. "Well, he didn't say no," she mumbled to herself and continued her search.

————

WHAT TAYLOR CAME UP WITH WAS AN EIGHT-YEAR-OLD DOG. WHEN she brought him home, he immediately greeted Grandpa with a sloppy lick to the face.

"Oh, you're a beauty," he said with a wide smile.

The dog weighed just over a hundred pounds and was a nice mix of black, brown and tan.

"His name is King, Grandpa."

He heartily rubbed the dog's head and neck. "Well, King, why didn't someone want you?" He looked up at Taylor.

"The previous owner had kids. King got tired of the kids jumping on him. Now that he's older it's getting hard for him to have patience."

"I find it hard to have patience with kids sometimes, too. Hope you like old people," he said and grinned.

It warmed Taylor's heart to see Grandpa happy about something. She went to her bedroom to finish packing boxes, getting ready for the big move. When she came back to the living room Grandpa was dozing, his hand touching King's back. King's tail thumped when he saw her.

She couldn't be happier with her choice of dog.

————

Taylor acquired a moving team from Boise. A man, woman, their daughter, and her boyfriend were happy to move them, since this was only their second moving job. She knew they'd work long and hard to get a reference for future clients.

Grandpa, sad and void of energy, sat in a lawn chair and watched the strangers move his belongings out of the home he'd shared with his beloved wife.

She decided to encourage Grandpa to wait to sell the house. Even though she considered a positive outcome with their new venture, she wanted him to believe he had an out.

Upon arrival, Taylor took a moment to study the exterior of their new home. Yet new was hardly the word for it, since the house was over a hundred years old. She thought it appeared kind of eerie, like the Addams Family residence, yet it didn't resemble the house. Her Queen Anne home, a three-story Gingerbread Victorian, had scalloped siding, decorative spindle rails and gables. The trim looked like wooden lace and was in fair condition.

The far-right side corner of the house was cylinder shaped all the way up the last story. Her realtor told her it was called a turret. There was a deck around the right side as well as one in the middle of the second floor.

When she bought this old mansion, she believed she'd gotten the deal of the century.

"This will be a remarkable house one day," she told a mover and he grunted in reply.

The house had a few broken windows and some of the inside walls would have to be torn down to the studs and completely rebuilt, but that was something Grandpa had done before. For that matter, she wouldn't mind using a sledgehammer herself.

Thank goodness, some of the hardwood floors were refinished and a few of the walls restored along with wood trims and moldings. She tried to put most of their furnishings in these rooms to ward off despair.

At dusk, when the movers took their leave, Taylor and King wandered through the house. It comforted her to have him nearby, since the house creaked and groaned with nearly every step.

Taylor found one door she couldn't open in one section of the house. Besides the door being locked, the light in the hallway was knocked out. From previously looking at the house from outside, it appeared to be behind the top floor deck near the tower room. Strange, she didn't remember this section on her preliminary tour and when King whined and scratched at the door, the hair went up on her arms. Something didn't feel right to her either. If she was not mistaken, she stood in a spot as cold as a refrigerator and she swore she could hear soft whimpering behind the door. Perhaps, she'd think about it tomorrow having had enough excitement for one day.

With her hands to her throat, she turned and nearly flew down the creaky stairs, with King in hot pursuit.

The following morning, getting ready for work, Taylor picked through boxes looking for her hair dryer. King followed her around from box to box, as if sure she had something in there for him. She took time to get him a dog biscuit as he'd earned his keep the first night of their stay. He'd slept on the floor at the foot of her bed, and she felt safe with him there.

"Now you take good care of Grandpa while I'm at school." She meant every word of it.

———

"WANT TO CATCH A MOVIE WITH ME THIS WEEKEND, TAYLOR?" TOM Getty asked. Today the school's physical education teacher dressed in a navy sweat suit, his wiry black hair cut short and combed back. She enjoyed his company in the teacher's lounge, and although handsome, he didn't push any happy buttons for her.

Dillon Nash however was another story. Even through the busy move, her mind would flash back to when she'd met him, the way he looked and presented himself. Yet how logical was that, since she'd probably never see him again? Perhaps it was good to hold a fantasy close to your heart when your life was a total mess, she guessed. She tried to banish him from her mind and concentrate on what Tom said.

"I guess your timing couldn't be worse. My grandfather is ill, and we've just moved into town. I really must focus on all that right now. I'm sorry."

In the space of a second, she saw what looked like disappointment, then embarrassment pass over his face. He collected himself quickly. "Oh, okay. Trillium Falls is a nice place to live. Where did you move to?"

"It's on Thayer Street. Maybe you've seen it, it's a Victorian house."

His eyes widened and he appeared to be speechless for a moment. "You've got more courage than I do."

"Well, yes it does need a lot of work but I'm hoping my grandfather will feel better soon and help me restore it."

"No, I mean the house's reputation." His shoulders went up and then he shook his head as if shivering. "I don't think I'd so much as enter it."

"What do you mean? I've heard nothing about a reputation." She mentally braced herself for bad news.

"You really don't know? How could you not know?" He pursed his lips then shook his head. "I'm sorry but I thought everyone knew the house is haunted. Some of the past owners have died there, rather mysteriously. Why the heck didn't anybody tell you that?"

Yes...why? she wondered. The new knowledge left her reeling like a paralyzing blow to the stomach.

Johnna Stevens, the school nurse, walked up behind them. "Hi, Taylor. Tom."

Tom looked uneasy. "Got to go. Talk to you later, Taylor."

She nodded at Tom, then looked at Johnna. Taylor needed time to process this information. She took a deep breath and tried to focus on Johnna.

Johnna and Taylor had hit it off since the first day of school when Johnna took time to welcome her. The freckles that stood out on her nose matched her ginger-colored hair. Her blue eyes large and animated when she spoke. "What did Mr. Getty want?" she asked with a wink.

"Actually, he asked me out," she answered, hardly above a whisper.

"Hmm."

"Maybe when my life settles down, I'll take him up on it." As if he'd darken her door now.

"You look like something is bothering you. Is your grandfather, okay?" She pushed back a few stray curls, then moved closer to Taylor.

"Thanks for asking; I appreciate it. He's not improving like I thought he would. He still wants to sleep all the time. No energy."

"You know I've been thinking about him lately. We had a student last year that was diagnosed with chronic infectious mononucleosis and since Gilby's meds are not kicking in like we'd thought, perhaps it's something like that. Or Chronic Fatigue Syndrome. Mono usually hits younger people, but it's worth a shot. Have him tested for the Epstein-Barr virus."

"You think so? I was thinking about taking him back in to the doctor, now I will."

"Do you still need some help moving? Paul said he'd like to help, and I could come stand in the way. I can't wait to see where you live."

"We moved last weekend. Thanks, but we hired movers from Boise. Now we can begin our new life." Or end it, she thought. Perhaps Grandpa *would* die in that house.

The first school bus arrived, and students headed to class, ending their conversation abruptly.

After school, Taylor stopped to pick up a few items at the grocery store on Main. "Thank you, Taylor," said the clerk, reading the name off her check. The gray-haired man wore a green apron over a protruding waist. He pushed his glasses up the bridge of his nose. "You're new around here, aren't you?"

Taylor nodded and he looked at her check again. "Thayer Street. Oh, is that that big Victorian?"

"Yes, it is." She waited for more unfavorable news.

"Are you going to tear it down? It's a very good lot in a good location. Worth building on again." He gave her a nice positive grin.

She supposed he meant well, but it only added another rung on her ladder of distress. "I'm thinking about it. That is, I'm still considering my options." She grabbed her groceries and fled before the clerk decided to enlighten her further.

Taylor sat in her car for a good ten minutes, struggling with the fears that brewed in the pit of her stomach. Overwhelming was the word of the day due to the house repairs, Grandpa's illness, and the rumors. But she wasn't alone, she reminded herself and the thought comforted her. Things would change when Grandpa was well again. He always knew what to do about everything. Until then it would be one day at a time, one project at a time. She could do it.

When she got home, she made a doctor's appointment for Grandpa, then looked on the internet for a roofing company.

"I think we have some time next week to start your roof."

First step done. She wanted to squeal with excitement. "Good! The address is 1215 Thayer Street. It's not far off of Main Street in Trillium Falls. You can't miss it; it's a large Victorian house."

"Oh. *Oh*...wait. I see I'm mistaken. We don't have any time next week."

"Well then, when?"

"Not for at least 6 months to a year."

"But you just said-"

"I'll be honest, ma'am. We've already been asked to put a roof on the house, but I can't get my people to go out there. They're afraid of the house."

Her heart started to pound. "But no one has to come inside. It's the roof that needs repair."

"They are afraid of falling to their death, ma'am."

Every roofing company in the area denied her. Boise didn't want to come the distance, although they would think about it if she paid a certain price, one she really couldn't afford.

Taylor went out to the front porch where King lay. His tail thumped when she sat down on the top step. She glanced up the three stories to the roof and wondered if she could learn to fix a roof. Long on determination, she liked to believe she could do anything; however, just looking up made her dizzy. She sighed. She certainly hadn't planned on Grandpa doing the roof, either.

As if King noticed her sad face, he nuzzled into her side. "It's nice to have someone care," she said to him, then hugged his neck.

She looked up to see Dillon Nash pull into her driveway and wondered what he could possibly want.

CHAPTER 3

Taylor got the house she wanted, but through the whole process felt of little significance, like a pawn in a pool of business sharks. She was a good person and hated being used that way. Even though Dillon hadn't been responsible for her woes, he was a reminder.

"Hello, Taylor."

King's tail thumped a greeting, destroying Taylor's concept of having a guard dog. She stood up and crossed her arms while she watched him walk from pickup to porch. He looked casual in a light blue Levi shirt and blue jeans.

"Dillon," she said with a nod. "What can I do for you?"

"I came to find out how you're doing."

"How I'm doing?" her voice rose of its own accord. "Why didn't anyone tell me about this house? I found out *today*, at school."

"The business world can be tough."

"The business world can be *tough*? I just got off the phone. I've been trying to get my roof fixed. Do you want to know the outcome?"

"I already know." He stuck his hands in his pockets, then looked up at the roof. "When I bought the house my real estate agent didn't tell me the history either."

It irritated her that even in her state of mind he appealed to her. She waved him off with a hand. "Don't you have some other business to take care of?"

"No," he said with a smile. His eyes were on her jumper. "You look like a teacher. The apples on your pockets give it away."

She brushed the front of her jumper off, in an attempt to end the conversation. "Look, I'm upset about the whole situation and seeing you is a reminder. I don't know what we have to say to one another, so if you'll excuse me."

"Wait." He held up a hand. "I want to help you put your roof on."

After standing with her mouth open for a few moments, she grasped at the hope of a solution to her problem.

"You want to help me put the roof on."

He chuckled. "No, I want you to hire me to do it. I don't need your help."

"Wait. How can this be, my realtor said you were from California?"

"I am, but I have business that'll keep me here for a while and I'm experienced with all kinds of carpentry. I'd like the job."

Taylor sat down on the top stair and absently looked at her shoes. She couldn't get her hopes up, just to see them fall. "Won't this be a big job for one person?"

"I can manage."

She let out the breath she'd been holding. "Okay."

He reached forward and she stood to shake his hand. Feeling some sort of tingling in her chest when their hands touched, she let go immediately.

Dillon simply turned and left.

No, this wasn't exactly the help she wanted, but she'd take it.

King moved toward her again and with a whine tried to lick her face, as if to tell her everything would be all right.

———

WHEN TAYLOR OPENED HER EYES THE NEXT MORNING, SHE SAW someone standing next to a window in her bedroom. A woman dressed in an 18th century style dress gazed out the window, yet the curtains were drawn. In one second, she disappeared, and Taylor wondered if she'd seen a ghost. Even though it was something Taylor had never experienced before, the figure didn't frighten her, only made her think she was part of a lingering dream. Something her morning coffee would soon remedy.

Later, in the teacher's lounge at work, Taylor set her lunch tray across from Johnna. "You're *good*, Johnna. You know your stuff. And I thought it was just depression."

"Oh, so my diagnosis was correct. Tell the administration how great I am since they keep cutting my hours."

"Yes, they listen to everything I have to say." Taylor looked around at the others in the room, her gaze resting on Tom for a moment.

"Well, naturally depression would be the first guess, since it followed the death of your grandmother."

Taylor nodded. "Yesterday the doctor gave me a scare. Do you remember sometime back, when I told you that Grandpa grabbed his side and fell, and I called 911? Anyway, since his side still aches, they were concerned about a ruptured spleen. It's okay though. And with his other symptoms - the sleep problems, sore throat, aching joints, the weakness and loss of appetite - he's a textbook case of mononucleosis."

"And the treatment is to be patient."

"Yes, right on, no miracle meds. They figure he won't be

completely back to normal for another two months. All we can do is treat the symptoms, and rest is the main remedy."

Johnna touched her hand in concern. "These are tough times for you, aren't they? Except, I know it's exciting to buy a house. At least you've got that."

"Yes, at least I've got that," she said, hoping Johnna would drop the subject.

As usual, Taylor's lunchtime went too fast. After recess, her students followed her down the hall like a mother duck and ducklings. She noticed tears on a girl's face and wondered if she'd be sending her to the office for ice.

When the students made a circle around the calendar, Taylor asked Katy what was wrong. "I heard my daddy say that you were going to die, 'cause, 'cause, you live in that yucky house. I don't want you to die, teacher," she said and burst into another series of tears.

All eyes shifted to their teacher. "Oh no, Katie. I will be fine. I have a great big dog to protect me."

"Are you a witch?" asked Jimmy.

"Now, do I look like a witch to you? Have you ever seen a witch with blonde hair? My job is to make that house pretty again."

"Are you a good witch like on *The Wizard of Oz*?" asked Jessica.

"No, I'm just an average teacher. I don't live alone; I live with my grandfather and of course my *great, big* dog. He looks like a police dog."

"I have a poodle and she protects me," added Jessica.

Like an actress, Taylor smiled and drew their attention to the calendar, but inside alarmed over what her students had heard.

After Taylor led her students to their bus, she found Johnna sitting at her desk. "Are you lost, Johnna? I think that's my desk. Or did administration decide to get rid of the nurse's room, too?"

"I'm sure that's coming. Listen, I've been wondering all day why you haven't told me about your haunted house?" asked Johnna.

"You know?"

"Everyone knows. Probably the president knows now, too."

Taylor leaned against the chalkboard. "I didn't want our conversations to be so serious. I hoped I could get away from my problems at work. Silly me."

"You want me to tell you a joke, or something?" Johnna asked with a smile.

Near tears, Taylor appreciated the humor.

"You know I'm not from Trillium Falls, I commute, so I guess I don't know everything about this town. Only their diseases," she said and made Taylor chuckle. "Anyway, I think you ought to go to the library and find out about the history of the house. I mean its *beginning*. It's a historical home and maybe you should just concentrate on that."

"You know, that's a good idea, Pollyanna."

"Well, that's the best I can do. No meds for this ailment either."

Taylor nodded. "Tell me what you've heard."

"Well, that three people died in the house. Two were involved in a suicide pact and one was said to have died from a heart attack. And Pollyanna that I am, I think the projection was correct. Yet, the people of this town think it was caused by something mysterious." Johnna threw up her hands in a questioning motion. "That's all I know."

"Huh. Guess I'll have to call a ghost hunter or something," Taylor said sarcastically.

"No, didn't hear anything about any actual ghosts."

"Does my house scare you?"

"No, I've been medically trained," she said with a smile.

Taylor appreciated Johnna's sense of humor and it felt good to leave for home with a smile on her face.

CHAPTER 4

When Taylor got home, she found Dillon in the front yard gazing up at the roof. King stood next to him sniffing a pant leg.

She stepped out of the car and King wagged his tail so hard he danced. After she grabbed her book bag, she walked over to Dillon and gazed at the roof as if she knew what to look for.

"Hi, Taylor. What did your students learn today?"

Again, his presence reminded her that she got the bad end of a business deal, and it was hard to feel positive. "That I'm not the good witch from *The Wizard of Oz.*"

"Excuse me?"

"Oh, never mind. You didn't leave me a cell number. I didn't know how to reach you."

He turned to face her. "Something wrong?"

"No, it's just that if I'd changed my mind, I wouldn't have had any way to reach you."

"Have you changed your mind?"

"Well, no. It's just that I thought about doing it myself." There, that was giving him an easy way out if he wanted one.

His eyebrows shot up, but he didn't respond. She looked down at his white, long-sleeved shirt. He did not look prepared to start work.

She took a deep breath and wondered how she could feel angry one minute, wanting him as far away as Timbuktu, then in the next moment think how good he looked in that shirt. Her feelings amazed her, and she decided she'd have to have Johnna diagnose this one.

"Specifically, why are you here?" she asked as professionally as she could.

"I'm here trying to figure out what I need to get for the roof. Not quite sure on the cost until I pick up the supplies." He turned and looked her in the eye. "I'll have a bid on paper tomorrow and if you agree, I can start same day."

He was her only help, so she didn't really have any power here, it was a simple as that. "Okay."

He wrote something on a scrap of paper, and she asked, "Do you need money to purchase the supplies?"

"No, I'll add it to the bill. You can pay me at the end. Is black okay for the shingles?"

"Yes, I think so."

Grandpa opened the front door and King ran to him. They all joined him on the porch. "This is my grandfather, Gilby. Grandpa, this is Dillon Nash, the gentleman who will be helping us with the roof."

Taylor stuck her hand out, so they couldn't shake hands. "Grandpa has mono," Taylor said happily. Grandpa looked pleased, too.

Dillon dropped his hand and looked at her through squinting eyes. "What?"

"Oh, the doctor recently gave us a medical diagnosis. He hasn't been doing well for a while now and we're just happy the doctor finally figured this out. He'll be back to normal in a few months. Right, Grandpa?"

"I'll not be kicking the bucket just yet, unless this grand-daughter of mine drives me to it."

"I think I can understand that Mr. Glenn," Dillon said with a smile directed at Grandpa. She wondered how she should take that when he added, "I'll be coming tomorrow to start on the roof and hopefully the weather will cooperate."

"You know that's a mighty big job for one man. No offense, but I told Taylor she should have gotten a roofing company to do it, but she wouldn't hear of it. Must be because you're so handsome and all."

Taylor could feel a blush coming on. Dillon didn't look pleased; probably because she hadn't told Grandpa the real reason she didn't hire a roofing company.

"I'm highly qualified, sir," he said. "I'm going to be tearing a lot off the roof and it will fall around the house. I'll get a dumpster for the debris. Hopefully, it won't fall too far into the berry bushes out back."

Grandpa nodded.

Dillon turned to leave. "I'll probably be here around two or three each day and work until dark. Goodnight."

Taylor watched him walk to his truck. However thankful for his help, her feelings were on her sleeve whenever he came around. Dillon was too darn good looking, and her body responded to him whenever he came close. So, naturally, she wanted him to be done each day by the time she got home. Yet, if he started work in the after-noon hours, he would only have about two or three hours of daylight to accomplish anything, consequently stretching out his involvement in her life for many days. She looked up at the roof and sighed.

Grandpa looked at her skeptically. "You're not getting up on that roof, Taylor."

He was right to make that statement, knowing her new determination to see a plan come to fruition. "Grandpa, it wouldn't do any good if I did, because I wouldn't know what to do when I got there." After a moment she said, "Why do you think Dillon's helping us?"

"Oh, let me sit down. Can't even go out onto the porch without getting winded. I think he sees a beautiful young woman in need. Gets the testosterone going every time."

Taylor felt her face redden again. Taylor doubted Dillon wanted her, he was all business today. She supposed he felt guilty for selling this white elephant of a house to her, but the most logical reason was that he needed the job.

"Sure, Grandpa."

To be honest with herself, she had mixed emotions. On the flip side, with no help available, it felt good to have a plan for the roof.

Taylor didn't look forward to cooking dinner in a partially unpacked kitchen. She noticed a large dark spider on the porch and carefully walked around it on her way inside.

———

ON ROUTE TO A BUSINESS MEETING, DILLON CONSIDERED WHAT AN alluring mystery Taylor turned out to be. Why hadn't she told her grandfather about how difficult it was to find help in this town? Basically, he'd thought that they were a team, especially since they both signed the papers on the house. Obviously, he was mistaken. So, it seemed to him that she worked alone. Albeit, she would have to be working alone since Gilby was a sick, elderly man. Why would a petite woman like Taylor want to take on a project like the haunted house of Trillium Falls?

Perhaps he hadn't considered these two characters thoroughly enough. True, Taylor and Gilby couldn't get help in town because of the history of the house, but why were they there in the first place? It seemed too illogical to believe them ignorant enough to think a helpless old man and a young woman, afraid to get dirty, could renovate this house. He shook his head and chuckled. After their time together in the basement, Taylor reminded him of a cat shaking her feet after stepping into something wet.

So, why would someone take such a risk? Financial gain came to mind. Yet, even if Taylor could rebuild this house stick by stick, she couldn't get her money back out of it on selling. He wondered if he'd missed something in the history of the house that could have caused her to think this was a good investment. *Only if she's a vampire*, he thought with a smile.

The only exception he could think of would be if someone came from a high-cost real estate area in California, wanted to pay less on a Queen Anne house in Idaho, and didn't know the history of the house. He knew that from experience.

Since none of this made sense, he wondered if somehow, she had learned about his wealth and set out to make a connection with him, and his pocketbook, by purchasing his house. No, he wasn't totally paranoid, other women had tried before in less fanciful ways. Yet, even if Taylor did know about his wealth, she didn't ask him for help, he offered to help her. He doubted anyone could be that clever because she'd have to know the average male would run the other way after looking over her situation. Also, she'd made no flowery excuses for her life circumstances to try and make him turn back to her.

Deep down, Dillon wanted to think of Taylor as a naive, defenseless young teacher doing all she could to help her grandfather get well. That was one of the reasons he wanted to help her in the first place. To all appearances, she seemed to be a passionate woman for those she cared for. It was against his beliefs that a woman like that should be walking around, without direction, on top of a steep roof. Especially with all the rest of the stuff she had to deal with right now.

Did he even know anyone her age who'd take in an elderly member of their family? Hell, he'd forgotten there was anyone left like her in this day and age, and it was pleasing to him. He'd never dated a woman like her before.

He planned to keep his word and finish this job; at the same time, he'd watch her like a hawk because he wouldn't be duped by a woman again.

THE FOLLOWING DAY, TAYLOR CAUGHT DILLON STANDING NEXT TO his truck, a cell phone between his ear and shoulder and a laptop computer in his hands. She looked up and saw scaffolding holding sheets of plywood for the roof. Then, for more than a moment, her eyes fixed on the hole in the thigh portion of his tattered work jeans.

"I'm not getting paid by the hour, if that's what you're worried about," he said to her matter-of-factly.

"No, I wasn't thinking that at all." She closed her jaw and decided to head for the house.

"Taylor, when you get a chance, I could sure use some water."

She turned around and he gave her a sugary smile. No need to charm her, she would have gotten it anyway, at least for the chance to see the hole in his jeans again.

On the way in the door, the rose bushes reminded her that she hadn't seen Calvin since day one. She turned to see that Dillon had finished his phone call.

"Dillon?" she called out, then walked toward him. "Do you know where Calvin goes in the evenings?"

"Well, the bewitching hour hits him about four or five o'clock and then he spends most of the evening passed out on his couch."

"Really?"

"Don't worry. I think he's pretty harmless."

"Things are supposed to get better," she said to herself as she approached the porch. She took a deep breath to calm herself before she opened the door to her grandfather.

A news program blared on television. She greeted Grandpa with a kiss on the forehead. Upright a little more often, she noted, pleased. "Your color is better today."

"You know, I think I feel a wee bit better, too," he returned with a smile.

"I want to go to the library. I think I'll go tomorrow if you think you'll be all right. If I fix you something to eat in advance, do you think you can manage?"

"I think so. You can't be my nursemaid all the time. Can't get you married off that way," he said with a twinkle in his eye.

"Yes, I'm sure my knight-in-shining-armor will be at the county library. Hey, has Calvin been over yet?"

"I haven't heard anybody at the door, but that doesn't mean he didn't knock."

She thought Calvin would want to meet him, especially since he mentioned they could be friends. Now she knew why he didn't come around in the evenings.

Outside, she couldn't find Dillon. She looked from the water bottle in her hand to the roof, then slowly and carefully maneuvered up one of the tallest, but sturdiest, ladders she'd ever seen. When she got to the top, Dillon saw her he slowly said, "Oh...no."

On his hands and feet, he maneuvered to the ladder. In anger, his eyebrows curved and drew together, reminding her of a Christmas grinch. "Hold still." He took the bottle. "Take the ladder with both hands. Now get down slowly and don't ever do that again."

Righteous anger hit her immediately. The ladder was secure, and she was only trying to help. *How dare he talk to her like that?* "I'm not exactly a China doll, Dillon, and thank you very much for the water."

He chugged the icy water down, then put a hand over his eyes.

Obviously, he had a headache from drinking the water too fast. She smiled, but decided she'd better get down before he started to yell at her again.

Dillon was right after her. In only a moment, they reached the ground and he handed her the glass of ice cubes. "Thank you for the water, Taylor," he said in a calmer manner, then put a hand up to his forehead again. "But please wait until I touch ground to give water to me in the future, okay? It makes me crazy to think of you up there."

She crossed her arms. "Just because I'm small, and a woman, doesn't mean I can't climb up on the roof. I could be of help to you."

"It's too dangerous up there. One of the reasons I'm here is because I was afraid you'd try to fix the roof yourself."

"Huh."

He jabbed a finger in the air. "I'm right, aren't I?"

She couldn't help but roll her eyes and point her finger back at him. "Hey, when you're finished here, I have some C batteries that need to go into my flashlight."

He frowned.

King joined them and he danced around the two with an occasional bark, sure something good was happening.

"Stop, King. It's my business what I do or don't do, Dillon."

He held a hand up. "Just please, don't be getting up on the roof again, okay?"

"You're not the boss of me." She couldn't believe she mimicked what she'd heard a first grader tell a classmate earlier in the day. Finally, in frustration, she said, "King, you're supposed to attack him, not play with him."

King jumped excitedly on her at the sound of his name, and she fell hard into Dillon's chest. He steadied her by bringing an arm around her back.

She looked up into brown eyes and in only a matter of seconds her brain turned to mush, she felt the ground moving under her, and she wanted to lick Dillon as bad as King did. Yet, the earth steadied when he set her firmly back from himself.

"King, no! Sit." King obeyed Dillon immediately, then watched and waited for the next command. Dillon gave her a visual perusal, she noted, as she sought her balance.

"Well, I wish King would do that for me," she said, nervously raking her hair with her fingers. "I...*we* have only had him for a little while."

"He still might be confused about who his owner is. You're gone at work during the day and Gilby can't give him a lot of attention. Oh, I've got you all dirty." He attempted to brush the front of her blouse off and then jerked his hand back as if he'd touched an open flame. He shook his head and chuckled to himself. "Sorry."

"Sure." She batted at her chest to remove the dust, while at the same time jiggling her ample flesh. His eyes followed her hand movements. A sound came out of him that could only be described as a half sigh and half moan.

"Uh...I'm getting back to work. Promise me you'll stay off the ladder, okay?"

Taylor thought about it for a moment, then looked at him out of the corner of her eye and nodded. She meant to tell the truth, but who was to say whether she might need to get on a ladder for some reason or other?

"Come on, King," she said.

King looked over at Dillon. "Go, King!" Dillon ordered. And he did.

CHAPTER 5

*V*isions of Dillon came to Taylor's mind, unbidden, several times during her workday. She thought of the moment in his arms, thanks or no thanks to King, and she flashed on his eyes and lips. She also wondered if he thought about her in the same manner, then mentally shook her head.

She sighed, then told herself it was simply because she hadn't been in close contact with a man in quite a while and that no red-blooded female would react any differently. He was very attractive, after all.

It was a good thing she planned to go to the library after school since she didn't know if she could face him today. Moreover, the next time she did see him, what would she say?

After driving twenty miles, the librarian pointed her to a machine where she prepared to view old newspapers on micro-film. News of her haunted house awaited her, and she'd find out all she needed to know in just a few minutes.

She put her purse down, got settled, and then her heart started to pound. She didn't like the feeling. If scared now, she'd be frightened even more if she found information to fuel her fears. Johnna was right, she needed to concentrate on the positive. Turning away, she thought of her big, potentially beautiful house and on that she'd focus.

Instead, she checked out an arm full of restoration books and felt darn good about the turn of her thoughts.

IT WAS WELL PAST DARK WHEN TAYLOR ARRIVED HOME. SHE FOUND Grandpa sitting on the couch, dressed for bed. His thin white hair stood up comically. If she was not mistaken, she spotted a sack from the local hamburger stand at his side.

"What's this?" she asked.

"Dillon thought maybe I was hungry."

"Didn't you tell him I had something for you in the kitchen?"

"No, I didn't say."

Taylor sat down next to him. She saw that he'd eaten most of his hamburger. He obviously felt better today. "Well, that was nice of him."

Curious about the tower room, Taylor went to the second floor and walked to the door. The light bulb she'd replaced in the hall, made it easy to examine the lock. She grabbed the keys from her purse and once again tried to find the right fit. King sat at her feet and sniffed at the bottom of the door while he waited for her to open it.

No, she didn't make a mistake the first time, not one key opened the lock. No one was coming in or going out, rest assured. It needed a new doorknob anyway.

"Taylor?" She could barely hear Grandpa's faint voice from the stairs.

"What, Grandpa?" She walked back to where he sat, with King right behind her.

"I said Dillon was kind of upset because you weren't here today."

All thoughts of the tower room fled. She lifted her chin. "Upset? Why?"

"Oh, he said something about your common sense." He looked at her out of the corner of his eye.

"What did I do?" she asked with a resigned tone.

"He came in at dusk, turned the lights on and wanted to know if I'd eaten and then he wanted to know why you weren't here helping me."

"Did you tell him I was at the library?"

"Yes, I said you were meeting someone special at the library."

"Grandpa! I was kidding about the knight-in-shining-armor part. Now, you know that."

"Oh well, I must have forgotten. I've been sick, you know."

"So that's when he went and got the hamburger?"

"No, that's when he got me into my pajamas."

"You haven't needed help getting into your pajamas for probably two weeks."

"Guess I was a little tired tonight." Once again he gave her that look she'd become accustomed to seeing over the years.

Should she be mad or happy? Clearly, Grandpa was bored, and had a little fun at her expense. Taylor covered her mouth with both hands to hide her smile.

However glad he had his sense of humor back; she'd wished he hadn't involved Dillon in this way. Maybe Dillon would forget about it by tomorrow, if not she'd deal with it then.

"Oh, Grandpa," she feigned exasperation and then walked into the kitchen to get herself something to eat. Suddenly she had an appetite. Despite Dillon, they were going to get back to normal and have a great house and a great life.

When Taylor arrived home the next day, she met Dillon coming down the ladder and she smiled sweetly. When he didn't smile back, but gave her a perturbed look, she lifted her chin and crossed her arms.

"How is Gilby doing today?" he asked, rather cynically she thought.

"Well, I was about to see. If you'll excuse me."

He took hold of her hand. She wasn't expecting it and stopped so fast she almost got whiplash. "You should keep your affairs at home, that way you can keep an eye on Gilby at the same time."

She frowned, "Well I can hardly teach my class from this house, Dillon."

"I'm talking about your sex life."

"Excuse me, what makes you think I have a sex life?" she ground out.

"You look pretty healthy to me," he answered while his eyes perused her body.

"As if this is any of your business, but since you're going to be here every damn night, I'll have to tell you that even though I wish I were having sex, I'm not."

What did she say? More time spent with Dillon, more mush in the brain. At least her words calmed his anger. He stared at her a few moments, then covered one eye with a gloved hand and continued to stare at her with the other.

"Now, please. I'm trying to calm down. We need to be professional with each other. I know you're concerned about my grandfather's care, but I think he played us both for fools last night. You see, he has a great sense of humor and he got bored and-" She stopped when she noticed Dillon's eyes on her chest.

"Anyway," she began again, re-crossing her arms, "I had dinner already fixed. It was in the refrigerator, and he could have gotten it himself. Also, he's been dressing himself for the last two weeks, so he really didn't need any help with his pajamas. I was gone only one part of an evening. Do you understand?"

"I'm afraid I don't understand at all, Taylor. I just don't want him dying here when I'm the only one around."

His rude comment piqued her anger. "So, you're saying when I want sex I should have it here, so Grandpa won't die alone?"

"That's pretty much it."

She wanted to slap him silly for his critique on her grandpa's care but thought better of it since she needed him to fix her roof. "Why don't I just come out and get *you* when I want sex, then I'll always be here, safely at home."

When he held a hand up, she continued, "Oh, I know! Yes, I will stay off the ladder!"

Dillon took a deep breath and steadied himself. "I'm sorry, but there is hardly enough daylight for me to have time to fix the roof, let alone stop and have sex, then get back up on the roof. I'm also sorry we've had this conversation, it's not my business." Dillon turned back to the ladder and left her standing with her mouth open. He left her angry again and physically frustrated all in one neat little package.

She met her grandfather at the door when he let the dog out into the yard. King ran right past her to Dillon. "Hello, Grandpa," she barked out.

"Having some trouble with the hired help, are we?"

"Yes, we are. But nothing a little spill off the roof won't fix."

She went directly to her bedroom, changed into jeans, grabbed a level and a screwdriver, and began the process of installing a towel rack in the second-floor bathroom. She needed something to get her mind off Dillon. Luckily, she had plenty to do.

After an early dinner, she went back to unpacking, searching for boxes containing unit materials for her first-grade class. The strong steps coming up the stairs told her Grandpa had gained some strength. She turned around with a smile.

Her smile quickly faded when she saw Dillon standing in the doorjamb.

. . .

DILLON WANTED TO REMIND TAYLOR OF HER RESPONSIBILITY TO Gilby when he'd walked into her bedroom. After helping Gilby last night, Dillon no longer felt she was an innocent young woman doing her best to keep a loved one alive.

She sat on the floor next to a box, unpacking, legs spread wide in a sexy pose. The room held a flowery scent, one he now associated with Taylor, and he couldn't help but take in a gulp of it. Over her head, he spotted a full-size bed and, since he no longer believed she was innocent, wondered how long it would take him to sleep in it.

It had been many years since a woman had been able to draw this type of reaction out of him, not since his teen years to be exact, and he didn't like it one bit. Obviously, there was something mystical about her or else he wouldn't be working on her roof. He tried to focus on the cracks in the bedroom wall, so he'd be able to walk out of the room.

"Gilby said you wanted to see me."

NO DOUBT, GRANDPA WAS AT IT AGAIN. DILLON WAS GOING TO think the two of them raving lunatics if he didn't already. Silently she searched her brain for something to say.

"He said you were concerned about my safety on the roof."

She had to smile. "I guess I did say something about the roof to him. No, I trust you'll be safe on the roof, I'm sure he must have misunderstood my words." She pushed a box of school supplies away from her and stood up, dusting her hands off on the legs of her jeans.

"I'm sorry about our conflict earlier. I'm truly thankful you are working on the roof. Right now, I don't know what I'd do without you."

He smiled a most appealing smile and she felt butterflies in the pit of her stomach. She put her hand there to still them and asked, "Are you hungry? Would you like to eat something?"

"No, I want...I need to get going. I've got some business to attend to and someplace to go. If that's all, I'll be going. Goodnight."

Instantly he vanished, leaving her to wonder if she dreamed the interaction. No, if it was a dream he would've stayed at least for a sandwich. To remain sane, she reminded herself he could've stayed, but chose instead to go somewhere else this evening.

———

KING SLEPT IN TAYLOR'S ROOM EACH NIGHT AND SHE APPRECIATED IT as noises increased. Whether it was the house settling, the wind blowing branches against the house, or even Casper, she didn't know. Even though doubtful as to the measure of protection she would receive from King, she didn't worry as much with him around. She'd be okay as long as he didn't bark, because barking meant someone, or something lurked nearby.

When Taylor woke Saturday morning the sun shined brightly through the lace curtains of her bedroom. She wondered how old they were and how long since they'd been cleaned. The house created enough work for her to do for the next twenty years.

She looked about the room and didn't spot King, meaning Grandpa was awake. Out the window she saw King chewing on a limb of a budding bush, while Calvin tried to chase him away. Taylor couldn't help but smile at the hubbub, because King seemed totally perplexed about what Calvin wanted. He danced around Calvin, excited with the game of it all. She decided she'd better get dressed and save Calvin and the bush.

In the closet she found a dress on the floor. She thought it strange as she knew the gown was hung securely enough with the rest of her dresses. After a moment, she pulled an outfit from the closet and dressed, then left the room.

Calvin, glad to see her, marched over to her like one of her students ready to tell on a playmate. "Your dog is going to ruin the plants, Miss! He's bothering the Daphne bush this morning and I'm noticing the pansies are getting trampled. I only planted them a few days ago. How can I do my job if this…this animal- Get down!"

Taylor tried to use a Dillon-like tone of voice with King. "Sit!" It surprised her when he did. Now what was she going to do? When she dealt with her students, she would just separate them. She pointed to the porch. "Go!" Again, surprisingly, he obeyed. Maybe she had the hang of it after all. She smiled at Calvin, but he was too upset with King to return it.

"Listen, Calvin, we're still working on training King. He's an eight-year-old dog, but he seems to have a few bursts of rowdiness left in him. But he's very good in the house, and most of the time he's calm. I'm sorry he upsets you, but I hope you will try to make friends with him. He's company for Grandpa and I feel comfortable with him around."

Calvin said nothing in reply. He lifted his cap and rubbed his crew cut, then his eyes narrowed to slits as he glared at King.

"You'll have to make peace with the arrangement if you want to live here."

Calvin visibly relaxed. "Oh, yes, I still want to live here, Miss. I've just never been too fond of dogs." He smiled then took a deep breath. "Nice day, huh?"

"Yes, it is. How long have you lived here?"

He eyed her suspiciously, she thought.

"About four years?"

"Do you know anything about the locked door on the third floor?"

"Now, I made sure no one could get into the tower room. I

changed the lock to the entrance. I caution you to stay out of there. I'm not going to unlock it; I'll tell you that right now."

So, she learned that the door led to the tower room. Somehow, she thought the turret on that side of the house was only a decorative piece of architecture, maybe closed off, and backed to a closet. She was even more anxious to see it now.

Taylor wondered if Calvin tried to scare her because he was mad about King. Whatever the reason, she decided not to ask any more questions. At least, not now. "I'm not asking you to open it, Calvin."

After a moment, she said, "I'm going to take King with me for a hike today. Maybe that'll burn up some of his energy."

"Thank you, Miss, I'd appreciate it."

"Hello!"

Searching for the voice, Taylor looked out across the yard to where a man vaulted over the back fence. King bounded from the porch to welcome him. The stranger stopped to pet King's head, then continued to where they stood.

He stuck out a hand to Taylor. "Hi, I'm Jerry Garcia. I'm sorry I haven't made it over sooner to meet you."

"Hello, I'm Taylor Glenn and this is Calvin Sweeney. It's nice to meet you." Taylor thought for a moment that Calvin wasn't going to shake his hand, but then he did.

"Nice dog. What's his name?"

Calvin let out a quiet, "Humph."

"His name is King," she replied, taking King by the collar to keep him from sniffing Jerry.

Jerry looked to be in his mid to late twenties, with unruly brown hair pointing in all directions. The thin man sported a red goatee. "I heard you're a teacher over at the grade school."

"Yes, first grade." *Word travels fast in a small town,* she thought.

"Are you two related?"

"Sure, we're married," Calvin said without any humor.

Taylor chuckled nervously. "Calvin, no relation, tends the grounds for me. He lives in the adjoining apartment." She pointed to his door. "My grandfather and I live here."

"And the man that works on the roof, who is he?"

"I hired him to do the roof."

"Is he from a roofing company?"

She started to feel like she was getting the third degree and felt uncomfortable. "No, he's the former owner."

"What do you mean you hired him?" Calvin cut in. "Perhaps you mean he has to do the repairs for the house to be up to code. You know, for selling purposes."

"No, we bought the house as is. I hired him to do the work. We all need to work for a living."

Calvin shook his head and gave her a look of disbelief. "As you say, but the man is a wealthy land developer."

Taylor, confused, was at a loss for words and Jerry's eyebrows rose in response. She'd think about this later. "Well, Jerry, what do you do for a living?"

"I work at a nursery. I know all about plants. If you want to know anything about them let me know," he said with a smile directed at Calvin.

"I haven't seen you around," said Calvin.

Calvin made Taylor uncomfortable and obviously Jerry, too, because he turned to leave. "Well, I'm pretty new to the neighborhood myself, and I work nights and sleep during the day. So, welcome to the neighborhood. I'll stop in and meet your grandfather one day soon."

Upon entering the house, Taylor found Grandpa in the kitchen. He'd been looking out the window at the three of them.

"Who was that?" he asked.

"A guy named Jerry. He lives behind us and he's welcoming us to the neighborhood."

"That's nice. Got a guy in your backyard and a guy on your roof. What do you think about that, young lady?"

"I think Jerry would not interest me if he were the last man on earth, however nice he may be."

Jerry was not on her mind, Calvin was. "Calvin was upset with King. He's been bothering some of the plants, I guess."

"Well, I think that's kind of good. Keeps me entertained watching the two of them go at it. Oh, he should be glad King's not a puppy. Right, King?"

King whined and thumped his tail.

"Have you met Calvin yet, Grandpa?"

"No. If I make any noise coming out the door, he's gone like a bat out of hell."

"That's strange."

"He might be strange. Well, think about it. He's living here alone in the maid's quarters, and it appears from my window watching that the plants are his only life."

"Dillon says Calvin has a drinking problem."

"That could explain it then. Probably doesn't want anyone around bugging him about it, or more than likely he's lost his family because of it."

"Yeah, I don't know about the stories he dreams up, too," she added.

TAYLOR SEARCHED THROUGH HER CLOSET FOR HER HIKING BOOTS SO she and King could visit the renowned Trillium Falls. It was such a beautiful day, too nice to stay in and unpack. The boxes would wait as King could use a walk and some bonding time with his owner.

When she drove to the falls, she made a special effort to absorb the changes that nature brought in this month of March. Taylor could see the beginnings of new growth on the fir trees, making the ends of the branches a spring green color. She doubted she could find a more beautiful place anywhere. Besides an abundance of pine trees, and a few cedar trees mixed in, she noticed the wild roses beginning to bud. The rose-colored flowers would be scattered ubiquitously into the region before too long.

Taylor followed the signs and pulled into the parking lot. King's tail wagged so hard she nearly fell over, and he licked her on the side of the face as she came back to take the keys from the ignition and put them in her pocket. After tying a hooded sweatshirt around her middle, she was ready to go.

The radio announcer predicted a temperature of sixty-five degrees with wind gusts. She'd be thankful for a breeze when she started hiking along the trail and working up a sweat. The wind blew at her in a hundred different directions making her glad she'd pulled her hair back in a ponytail.

Instantly, King was off and running with Taylor dragging behind, his one-hundred-plus pounds too much to handle. Too late she realized she should have tested the dog and leash before she'd decided to go far from home. She now knew whose energy was going to be expended and it wouldn't be his.

"King. King. King!" A charging German Shepherd was frightening to say the least, and she certainly didn't want to scare anyone. Every tourist had to be sniffed, then greeted. Thank goodness they didn't run into any other dogs. Disappointed, she decided to go home and see the falls another day.

Almost to the car, the leash slipped from her hand and King ran away. The thought of him chasing another dog terrified her.

Worse, he ran up to Dillon. Taylor's heart picked up a different kind of beat when she saw him, then calmed after realizing he was here with another woman.

Dillon motioned for the woman to go up ahead while Dillon brought King over to Taylor. He looked around her, into her car.

"Where's Gilby?" he asked, concern in his voice and a frown on his face.

It ticked her off, his thinking she didn't know how to care for Grandpa, yet she didn't want him to know it. "Oh, don't worry. It's his nap time."

"You know you should really hang on to King."

"Well, I'm not stupid, you know," she shot back, unable to control her feelings.

He didn't look convinced. Taylor grabbed the leash and, with all her strength, pulled a whining King over to the car. Dillon stood and watched until King was safely stowed away, then he nodded and sprinted over to the waiting woman.

Taylor couldn't help but stare. The woman was nearly as tall as Dillon, tan, blonde and long-legged. Her hiking clothes looked brand new and expensive. One thing she didn't have that Taylor did, was youth. She guessed the woman to be around forty.

Taylor felt a little disheartened. A lot disheartened and it had nothing to do with King. Suddenly, she realized she had a crush on Dillon and searched her heart trying to find out why. What she came up with was probably the truth. He was her knight-in-shining-armor. He took care of her roof when no one else would. He even cared about Grandpa.

Now, as she looked at the other woman, she wondered why Dillon helped them. Grandpa thought it was because of Dillon's attraction to her. Not likely, since she could see he already had a woman in his life. Was it really money, a job? Calvin didn't think so. Yet, it wasn't reasonable for a wealthy man to be repairing her roof.

Could it be guilt? Guilt because he'd sold her a white elephant that she'd never be rid of. It would do her good to ask him, and then maybe she could get a perspective on this. Only first graders believe in knights-in-shining-armor.

· · ·

ON MONDAY, TAYLOR DROVE HOME FROM SCHOOL WITH SWEAT ON her brow. Her stomach churned and her shoulders ached, making her realize she'd picked up the stomach flu at work, most likely from the student that threw up on her feet on Friday.

Now, the trek from her car to the bathroom seemed like a journey of awesome proportions. She pulled the keys from the ignition and looked up to see Dillon making his way to the driver's side of the car.

He was the last person she wanted to talk with right now. Instead, all of her mental energy went to making do in a pinch, perhaps throwing up in her washable book bag as an alternative to throwing up in her car.

Dillon opened the car door. "Hello."

When she only grunted, he said, "Do you need to me carry your bag for you?"

"No," she barely got out, and emptied the books onto the seat. She clutched the empty bag close to her chest and ducked under Dillon's arm draped across the door.

"Oh dear, oh dear," she said and took off mumbling like the white rabbit in Alice in Wonderland.

Apparently, she startled Dillon because he followed right behind her. Still clutching her book bag, she gave a quick wave to Grandpa, decided she shouldn't dirty his bathroom, and headed up the stairs as fast as her body would take her.

"Taylor!" Dillon said sternly, like she could stop if she wanted to.

"Please let me go, I'm sick!"

She heard him taking the stairs behind her.

"Please, please go away, I'm sick," she said, using up the last of her strength. After tossing her book bag to the side, she lifted the lid on the toilet and plopped down on her knees.

Dillon took a washcloth from a cupboard under the sink and turned on the water. After wringing out the excess water from the washcloth, he placed it across her forehead with one hand and when she stood up to heave, he took hold of her from behind giving her the strength to stand.

She wanted to push him away, but instead fell against him. "I'm dying," she said.

"Shush. You'll be fine."

That's when all hell broke loose; he tightened his hold and continued to press the washcloth against her forehead. It was the sweetest thing anyone had ever done for her.

"I don't want you to get sick," she said between gasps.

"I have a very strong stomach. Don't worry about me."

When the worst was over, he helped her to her bed and left. She'd dozed for a minute and when she opened her eyes, she found he had returned with a large stainless steel bowl that he put beside her bed.

"You should go," she said.

"I will, pretty soon."

"Why are you staying? You could get sick."

"I'm staying because you and Gilby need me to."

"You're a good man," she said on an exhale. Feeling helpless, her eyes filled with tears, making her glad the room was now dark.

CHAPTER 6

*W*hat woman wouldn't fall for a handsome guy that held her while she barfed? Still, Taylor needed perspective. Just because he was nice to her, cared for her when she was sick, didn't mean he wanted her for a girlfriend. As far as she knew, he was serious about the woman he took to the falls, a woman who, most likely, did not come with an ailing grandfather. She'd gone through this before with a man and didn't want to go through it again.

If that was not enough to send Dillon packing, he saw her barf, for goodness sake.

Dillon was indeed becoming her knight-in-shining-armor, and she had to nip it in the bud. She had to cool it, that was all, and act like nothing happened to her heart as he nursed her back to standing.

TAYLOR WAS PROUD OF HERSELF ON HER FIRST DAY BACK TO SCHOOL. In retrospect, she realized that she hadn't let herself think of Dillon all day. Now she'd get out of her car, go straight to the house and the rest of her day would go fine. Except before she stepped onto the porch, she heard a shrill whistle.

"Darn!" She stepped back and lifted her eyes while her heart gained a beat.

"Aren't you even going to acknowledge that I'm up here?" he shouted down at her.

"Oh, I didn't see you!" Well, that was true, she didn't look up.

"Yeah, right. I can see you're feeling better. You seem to have company, but I'd like to talk to you before I leave tonight."

She looked at the house speculatively and said, "Sure."

Inside, she found Grandpa and Jerry Garcia hovered over a game of checkers. It brought a smile to her face. "Who's winning?"

"Hello, Taylor," said Jerry. "I thought I'd have no trouble winning since Gilby's been sick, but no, he's quite the rival."

"How are you feeling, Grandpa?"

"I'm starting to get a little tired, but this has been fun. I'll just go to bed early tonight. Thanks, Jerry, for coming by and staying awhile."

"Would you like to stay for dinner, Jerry?" Taylor asked as she headed for the kitchen.

"Thanks, but remember I work nights. I'll be out of here shortly."

"Maybe some other time then."

What she envisioned was Calvin and Grandpa playing checkers, not Jerry. She listened to the light banter between the two men while she cooked a spaghetti dinner.

"Taylor, Jerry's father grew up in Montana, not far from where I grew up. How about that? Says he knows the area well."

"Well, that'll give you plenty of things to talk about."

Grandpa grew quiet and rubbed his face. Jerry, after watching him, said goodnight and took the back door home. Following their early dinner, Grandpa went right to bed.

While waiting for Dillon, Taylor picked up a magazine and

tried to read, but found it hard to do when she kept looking at the door and pushing back the cuticles on her fingernails.

After what seemed like hours, Dillon knocked quietly on the door. King greeted him warmly.

"Listen, can I come in a minute?"

"Sure."

He walked past her and stood next to the fireplace.

"Do you want something to eat or drink?" she asked.

"No, I want to run something by you, but I want you to sit down first."

She sat quickly in the chair by the door. "You're starting to scare me. What is it?"

"When I talked to Jerry Garcia, I had a bad feeling. I know it's none of my business, it's just that Jerry has phony written all over him-"

She stood. "What do you mean?" she interrupted, hand on chest.

"Well, his name is Garcia for one. He looks too Irish to be named Garcia. Jerry Garcia is the name of the late leader of the Grateful Dead rock group, and he looks exactly like a dead head groupie. He works at night for a nursery. Isn't that daylight work?"

She crossed her arms. Jerry did her family a huge favor by befriending her sick, elderly grandpa. "Huh. And don't forget he has a red goatee, but the hair on his head is brown."

"Okay, forget it. I only tried to warn you to be careful because you seem to have enough problems right now." He walked past her and opened the door.

She sat down and put her hands on her face. "Get a hold of yourself," she said aloud, and King thumped his tail. She let out a calming breath. "Come on, King, let's go upstairs and peel wallpaper."

. . .

DILLON STOOD WITH HIS BACK FACING THE DOOR, TAKEN ABACK OVER the conversation he'd had with Taylor. Yet, it was not only her words that troubled him, but the underlining tone of her voice. She appeared to trust everyone but him.

In frustration, he rubbed his face with his hands and then moved down the creaking front steps that reminded him the house was in dire need of repair. Repairs that would only be done if he did them, due to the cowardly state of the men in this town. How could she not need and trust him?

Maybe someone told her he didn't need the roof job or her money. Yet, even then, she should be nothing but grateful for his help.

Rain drops fell on his head and he wondered what insanity had possessed him to help this woman. It wasn't guilt. The guilt he felt for selling it to her subsided when he offered her a chance to back out. Any logical person would have taken it.

He was no Mother Teresa, but he did help the underdog from time to time. Dillon fully believed that to whom much is given, much needed to be given in return. He tried to tell himself the roof job was a work of charity, but in reality, it had more to do with the woman herself.

To dupe himself into getting near her, he'd painted a picture of Taylor that pointed to sainthood, even though her halo slipped from time to time when it came to watching out for Gilby. He wanted to find any excuse he could to convince himself that she was worth going after, because he found her incredibly sexy. Since she had a need for him, it made him feel masculine and all-power-ful, like there was nothing in the world he couldn't do.

When she didn't follow his lead about trusting Garcia, he felt frustrated and helpless not being able to help her. As a result, she gave him great highs and great lows. No way could this be the beginning of a healthy relationship. *So, what can I be thinking? Or better yet, what am I thinking with?*

.   .   .

WHAT A MESS THE WALLPAPER WAS. TAYLOR KNEW SHE NEEDED TO rent equipment to pull it off the walls, yet she started peeling at it with her fingers while she thought about Dillon, then moved to religion, politics, anything to get her thoughts off him.

King sniffed the peelings after they fell to the ground. "No, don't eat it. Drop it, King." King whined and went to the corner to lie down.

"Why would Dillon care about Jerry?" she asked King. King thumped his tail. "It's none of his business, right?" King's tail thumped again. "Dillon has a girlfriend. We're not really even friends, he just works for me. Why doesn't he go back home to California? Why is he staying to help me?"

King whimpered, then left the room. She smiled at the intelligence of leaving a frantic woman but froze when she heard him growling.

Taylor walked slowly into the hall and saw King, now barking, at the door leading to the tower room. She could feel goose bumps forming on her arms. With a hand, she tucked hair behind an ear but all she could hear was King. For good measure, she let him bark for a minute before trying to quiet him. He gave a low-pitched growl, and she still couldn't hear a thing. Her heart beat wildly when she reached for the doorknob while watching King, ready to spring. The door remained locked, so what else did she expect?

When King calmed down, so did she. It was probably a mouse. Still, for the rest of the evening, every creak, snap, and tick frightened her as well as the condition of the house, Grandpa's health, Calvin, Jerry and Dillon. Thank goodness for her job. At least she could trust her first graders.

.   .   .

The following morning, Taylor mentally kicked herself for not paying attention to what she was doing. She overcooked the bacon and broke three egg yolks she wanted to fry. She groaned, then picked out bits of eggshell and scrambled the eggs.

"Did you hear King barking last night, Grandpa?"

"Yes, I woke up a couple of times. I also heard someone talking. I think you had the TV up too loud. What was King barking about?"

The television wasn't even on last night. Realizing Grandpa heard her discussing Jerry with Dillon, she felt her cheeks redden. She turned to the stove so Grandpa couldn't see her face. "King was barking at the door that leads to the tower room."

"Probably a mouse or something. It wouldn't hurt to get a cat in this big old house."

"I thought it could be a mouse, too." Well, it was one of her thoughts anyway, but she wasn't going to upset him with her active imagination.

"I noticed that door is locked. Do we have a key for it?"

"No, we don't. The lock will have to be changed."

"Why don't you ask Dillon to change the lock? I still have some mad money around somewhere."

Taylor could do the job, she knew. It may take her awhile, but she could do it. One could find directions to anything on the web. She wished he would realize that she wasn't helpless. Yet, if it made him happy to have someone else do it, what difference did it make? Soon, he would see what she was capable of, and she'd be happy with that.

She turned around and crossed her arms over her apron. "Why don't you ask him?"

"Because I don't have as much energy as you do. I can't go out and chase him around."

She put a hand to her chest. "Are you insinuating that I'm chasing him around?"

"Maybe when you got up on the ladder. He told me about that. Doesn't want you on the ladder."

"He asked me to get him some water," she said, her voice rising.

Grandpa swallowed a piece of toast. "I thought we were having fried eggs this morning."

"We can't always have what we want."

"Now, I'm not in the first grade so don't treat me as such. Now what were we saying? Oh yes, so you were just being nice when you took Dillon a drink of water?" His eyebrows rose in question.

"Yes! I'm a very nice person." she answered sarcastically.

"God help your first graders this morning," he mumbled and picked up the paper.

————

SPRINKLES OF RAIN DOTTED THE WINDSHIELD AS TAYLOR MADE HER way home. *Dillon will probably be taking the afternoon off*, she told herself.

She was wrong. Through the windshield she could see him on the roof, pulling a sheet of plywood from the scaffolding. At least he had rain slickers on. She shook her head, glad she didn't have a job that required her to be outside no matter the weather. *Yeah right, he was rich.* Calvin had to be mistaken, because this was a man trying to make a buck if she'd ever seen one.

She felt a little sorry for him, then a little aggravated. Even dogs knew to get out of the rain.

"Why don't you come in until it stops raining?" she shouted up at him.

"It's just sprinkling. I want to get the rest of the plywood on the roof!" he shouted back.

"Just trying to be *nice*," she muttered to herself while she walked into the house.

"What, no checker partner, Grandpa?"

"No, and it's probably a good thing, I think I'm coming down with a cold. But I guess that's better than the stomach flu."

"Oh, no," she answered. Disappointed as much for herself as for Grandpa.

"I'm on my way up to take a nap. Wake me for dinner, that way maybe I'll sleep tonight."

"Yeah, sure." She watched him head up the stairs until the phone rang.

"Dillon Nash, please," came the male voice. She bit down on her lip, wondering if she should bother Dillon.

"Uh…"

"It's important. I tried to reach him on his cell but he's not picking up. My name is Jeff Clark."

"I'll try to get him."

She looked up into the rain. "Dillon!"

"I said I'm not coming down."

Was it the rain or her that frustrated him? she wondered. She put her hand up to her ear trying to signal that he had a phone call. "Phone call!"

He nodded and then she tried to go about business as usual. After attaching ears to her MP3 player, she proceeded with dinner.

When Dillon came to the door, King, tail wagging, followed at his heels to the kitchen. He touched her shoulder to get her attention and she removed her headphone. "Taylor, do you have a bandage? I nicked myself pretty good."

The gash startled her, but she moved quickly to get a paper towel. "Oh sure. Here, wash your hands. I'll tell Jeff you'll be right there."

"It's Jeff on the phone?"

"Yes."

Taylor grabbed an antiseptic gel, some cotton swabs, and Band-Aids. She came into the living room in time to see him pull his rain jacket off over his head, taking his shirt with it. He grabbed his shirt but was so immersed in what Jeff was saying that he didn't get it back on.

Taylor stepped back and stared at his muscular chest, biting her tongue to keep herself from whining like King. She could see the edge of his navy boxer shorts above his jeans. Then her eyes went to his lips and watched them go into that crooked smile that she'd started to find irresistible.

She laid the first aid products down next to him and stepped away, hoping to leave the room. Dillon lifted his hand wrapped in the paper towel. "Help?"

Queen of nice that she was, she sat down beside him on the couch and took his outstretched hand. "You want me to? Your finger?"

"Yes, just fix it like you do your first graders. Not talking to you, Jeff."

Without thinking, she picked up his finger, turned it away from the wound, and kissed it. Stopping in mid-sentence, he looked over at her, his eyes wide.

"That's what first graders want you to do." *Probably with less tongue though*, she thought to herself. She took a deep breath to calm herself, then proceeded to examine the small gash. It appeared to have stopped bleeding.

Taylor dabbed the wound with antiseptic gel, then put on a knuckle bandage. While studying his palms, she found several little gashes, but she highly doubted he wanted Band-Aids plastered all over his hands. The skin had hardened from exposure to the elements, and he kept his fingernails clipped short. A working man's hands.

Holding his hand seemed such an intimate thing to do. Up to this moment, she only dreamed of touching him and now she had the chance. Moreover, he'd even asked her to.

She looked up to see him staring at her, yet somehow looking straight through her while he spoke to Jeff. The hair on his head retained gold streaks from the sun, his shoulders a light bronze. It was nigh impossible for her to keep her eyes off his chest. A light scattering of brown hairs tapered down to his belt.

Dillon unconsciously took a hand and pushed back his hair revealing well-shaped arm muscles. His hair was partially wet, and a few raindrops had fallen on his chest. She wondered if he felt chilled and reached out to swipe at the raindrops. He placed his hand over hers before she could pull away and held it captive there.

"Are you sure, Jeff? Yeah, you're usually right. I'll look through my papers again tonight."

He wasn't cold. His skin was warmer than hers. She tried to wiggle her hand loose to no avail. "Listen, Jeff, how long will you be up tonight? I'll call you back later, hopefully with the numbers you want. Yeah, later."

Dillon set the phone down and looked at her with eyebrows raised in question.

"I was brushing the raindrops from your chest. I thought maybe you were cold," she said now a little embarrassed at taking the liberty.

"Move, King." He stood up and pulled off the rest of his rain slickers, revealing the jeans with the gaping hole. "Well, am I?"

Heavens, no, she thought. *He was hotter than hot.* "Uh…doesn't look like it."

"Where's Gilby?"

She pointed upward. "Taking a nap. I'll wake him for dinner."

Dillon sat back down and gently took a handful of Taylor's hair and watched it sift through his fingers.

She supposed he was allowed a liberty, since she took one.

"You know, I've been around several days now and I can see you're not seeing anyone seriously."

"Just Jerry," she said tongue-in-cheek.

Dillon's expressive brown eyes half closed when he smiled.

After a moment he asked, "Does that mean you're available?"

Who'd want to darken the door of her haunted house? Humph. "Uh...
I had a boyfriend, but it's over."

"And what happened to him?" he asked.

"We dated through college; things went well enough. Then
Grandpa needed me, and he didn't like the intrusion."

"Not many would, I guess."

"No."

After a moment of quiet, Dillon smiled. He slouched back and
his eyes briefly scanned her figure. Taylor shifted in her seat
uncomfortably.

When he said nothing, she could see he wasn't going to offer
any information about himself without a little coaxing. "How
about you? Are you seeing anyone seriously?" she asked, then held
her breath waiting for some information about the woman she'd
seen him with at the falls.

"I was. Until about," he counted on his fingers, "four months
ago."

"And?"

"And it didn't work out."

"Because?"

Dillon pushed his hair back, then grabbed his shirt and absently
gazed at it while he spoke. "She didn't really love me for me. She
loved me for my career and what I could buy her. She didn't even
have any goals, besides wanting to marry me."

Taylor doubted this was the real reason. His career? A carpenter? A roof guy? Certainly, a good occupation, but she didn't think
the job fit the scenario he was referring to. How could she put it
kindly? Maybe she couldn't. "Men sometimes misunderstand
women."

Dillon looked up from his shirt, his eyebrows furrowed. "I beg
your pardon?"

She pointed up and down his physique. "I can understand her

wanting you for your uh...looks, but not your job."

He pulled on his shirt. "What are you talking about?"

"I'm saying that kind of woman would probably be after someone who's a lot richer than you."

"But I am rich."

"Yeah, that's why you're doing my roof," she pointed upward.

Dillon's eyebrows went up and down about four times. Finally, he looked agitated, which made her believe she'd hit the nail on the head.

"Why do you have such a low opinion of me?"

"I...don't."

He threw up his hands and then pulled a candy bar from his rain jacket and broke it in half. "Here maybe this will sweeten you up."

Unconsciously, while considering his words, she took the chocolate he offered and began munching. After crossing her arms, she gave him a smug look, while King sniffed around trying to find escaping crumbs.

"Okay, Miss Know-it-all, so I'm not rich, huh?"

Taylor pointed at the rip in the thigh portion of his worn-out jeans. "Hardly."

"Well, I didn't think I should be out working in my best clothes." Dillon pulled at the hole making it larger.

The same reflex she used at school to interrupt a child from doing something he shouldn't came out instantly and she reached into the split fabric protecting it from his hand. What she found there was a warm, hard thigh.

Taylor nearly choked on her last bite of candy. He watched her lick her lips with her tongue. His eyes flickered, then dilated to nearly black.

Taylor tried to remember what they were talking about. It was tough but she finally remembered. "I am sweet," she said in a whisper.

Dillon's lips went over hers in a soft caress. When Taylor didn't pull away, he placed his hands on her face and kissed her again with greater intensity, searching out her tongue. "Maybe you are sweet," he said against her lips.

She felt herself being pulled onto his chest while he continued his descent down onto the couch. King met them there and proceeded to lick Dillon's face. Dillon pushed Taylor back to sitting position and wiped his cheek with the sleeve of his shirt.

"Now that's not sweet," he said to King and laughed. "You don't want to miss out on any fun, right buddy?"

At that moment, King left for the stairs.

Taylor realized Grandpa was awake. She self-consciously twisted a strand of hair around her finger, eyes locked on the coffee table.

"Taylor? Look at me." Dillon's eyes locked with hers. "Are we ever going to finish this?"

She wondered how she was supposed to answer that. She was enticed by him, albeit, but she questioned how smart an affair with him would be.

"I don't know. I really don't know anything about you and frankly the things you do tell me I find hard to believe."

He didn't have time to respond because Grandpa came into view, King at his heels. "Oh, smart man, Dillon, getting out of the rain."

"Are you feeling better, Grandpa?"

"A little bit, yes. Did you ask Dillon to replace that lock?"

"No...it...a...slipped my mind." Especially since, she'd hoped Grandpa would ask him. "We need to replace the lock on the door that leads to the tower room."

Dillon looked at Taylor and sighed, "Are you sure you want to get into that area of the house?"

"What's wrong with the tower room?" Grandpa asked Taylor in concern.

They'd broached the subject that Taylor didn't want Grandpa to know about. She didn't want him to worry, not until he was back to his old self again.

"Oh, nothing much," she said, and Dillon's eyebrows went up. Quickly she added, "I've heard that it needs some redoing."

"Well what little corner and crevice in this house doesn't?" Grandpa replied, astounded.

"Exactly. Now, Dillon, will you or won't you replace that lock?" Taylor crossed her arms as if to dare him to tell Grandpa anything negative.

Dillon crossed his arms as well. "Well of course I'll do it. I need the money."

Grandpa looked back and forth from Taylor to Dillon with thinned lips. "What's the problem here, Dillon? Do you need some money for roof expenses? We can do that if that's what you'd like."

Dillon held up a hand. "No. No. I will bill you at the end. No problem." He grabbed his rain slicker and headed for the door. "It's still raining. Uh, snowing now, so I'll just go pick up everything I will need for the door. Good night."

"Boy, Taylor, you can sure get that boy riled up. Ease up on him. Humor him. At least until we get the roof done. Wouldn't want him to stop midway."

"I don't think he's going to quit. You heard him; he needs the money."

Taylor walked toward the kitchen. She had trouble keeping her mind on dinner since her brain willfully focused on the kisses she'd shared with Dillon.

She couldn't remember any man controlling her thoughts, as much as Dillon. Today, she had no preparation for what'd happened to her, it was like riding on a roller coaster of emotions and every roller coaster ride she'd ever taken upset her stomach. Consequently, when dinner was finally done she could only eat a few bites.

CHAPTER 7

*I*t was Saturday and Taylor prepared to use her day wisely. She'd taken advantage of some sales and came home with everything she needed. Now ready, she planned to remodel her bedroom, trying some techniques she'd learned about in cream, beige, and light mauve.

Rising early, she swept her hair into a top knot designed to appear haphazard, donned an old pair of jeans and an old Mickey Mouse sweatshirt. Thankfully, the hardwood floors were smooth enough to slide furniture, on rugs, through the doorway.

Taylor sanded the ceiling so hard that she thought she might wear a hole in her gloves. Finally, when she swiped the ceiling with a rag and no residue remained, she added a clay base adhesive. She applied a white English relief paper wall covering up to the chalk line she'd used as a marker on the ceiling. The paper bore a pattern much akin to a snowflake design with a matte finish. When finished the ceiling would have an old-world elegance.

Because of the nicks and bumps on the walls, she chose glass weave wall covering. Once hung, she applied a texture compound and when finished dabbed the surface with a sponge making a nice even pattern.

She listened to a radio talk show and argued aloud with one of the women callers. *How could a person be so stupid about love?* she wondered. When she calmed down, she realized *she* could be stupid around Dillon, too.

Dillon kissed her. How interested was he? She chuckled. Yes, he kissed her, but what red-blooded male wouldn't respond to a hand on his thigh? Sheesh. She couldn't believe she'd done that. If she wasn't careful, she'd be calling in to the radio program.

Where was Dillon? It was after four o'clock and she hadn't heard any noise on the roof.

"Enough of that." She changed the channel and rock music filled the room. The music renewed her energy, and she danced a jig or two while sponging over portions of the first wall she'd finished.

King came in and tried to join her by nipping at her heels as she danced. Taylor laughed, exciting King even more. To keep him from biting too hard, she had to keep her feet still. She put her feet together, bent her knees, moved her seat back and forth and snapped the fingers of her free hand.

Taylor froze. She slowly stood up straight, bit down on her lip and turned to find Dillon propped against the doorjamb with arms crossed.

"How long have you been standing there?" she asked.

"Long enough." He smiled from ear to ear, then looked up. "The ceiling looks really good."

Taylor turned the music down. "You act surprised."

"I just didn't know you had this in you. But it looks nice. You should be proud."

She smiled. "I have a little moxie in me. Thanks, I hoped it would turn out nice."

His eyebrows furrowed. "What kind of adhesive did you use on the ceiling?"

"Clay base. I probably have some on my face if you want to see what it looks like," she said, then continued, "I thought this room was one of the easiest to tackle. I'll have to rent a steamer to get the layers of wallpaper off in much of the house."

Dillon walked around the room, then stopped and examined where she used a trim guard to cut against the molding. "Probably a good idea. Especially since Gilby can't help you."

"Oh, he'll help me." She turned in time to see a sympathetic expression cross Dillon's face.

"Taylor-"

She shot up a hand. "I will hear nothing to the contrary. He's the only family I have left. He's the reason I bought this place, to give him inspiration to live again and to have something productive to do. Grandpa and I are going to rebuild this place."

"*That's* why you bought this place?" He looked at her like she had lost her marbles. "Surely there are houses around here that don't need this much work."

"Nothing worth mentioning, but this house is a renovator's dream. It'll be beautiful when we're done."

The incredulous look he continued to give her grated on her nerves. She turned away and sponged over the same spot.

After a moment of silence, Dillon came up behind her, wrapped his arms around her shoulders and gave her a hug. He pulled away just as quickly and said, "I took the initiative and ordered a new doorknob, uh...handle for the door." He pulled a brochure from his pocket and placed it in her hand. "I thought you would probably want a style that would go with a Victorian house, so it had to be ordered."

The sympathetic hug caught Taylor off guard making it hard to focus on what he said. It took some effort to look at the pamphlet in her hand. "Oh yes, the door. Oh...okay."

"I'm going to California over the weekend. I'll see you Monday." He turned to go.

"Wait." She turned around and Dillon walked back to her. He stood about a foot from her. She read somewhere that most people liked a space of at least two feet between themselves and another person. She quickly decided she'd have to agree with the article since his closeness became a tad bit overwhelming. Her lungs took in his after-shave like a welcome breath of fresh air. He smiled and she almost shook from the hormonal impact on her body when their eyes connected for a time.

"Hey." He backed up, chuckled, and said, "Don't get the sponge on my clothes."

She felt somewhat embarrassed and tried to cover her awkwardness. "What makes you think I was going to touch you? Of course, I wouldn't get this goop on you."

"You were going to kiss me."

"I was going to kiss you?" Her sponge went to her chest putting texture compound across Mickey Mouse's ear.

"I know when a woman wants to kiss me, and you wanted to kiss me."

"*I* wanted to kiss you?" she asked again this time deleting Mickey Mouse's nose with the sponge.

Dillon looked down at her chest and backed up another step. "Okay, why did you want me to wait?"

"Oh, I wanted to know-" What did she want to know? She was lonely stuck up in this room all by herself, his company was nice, and she enjoyed the hug. She didn't want him to leave.

"Why California?" she asked as calm as she could.

"I live there."

"You're going home then?"

"For the weekend, like I said." For some reason Dillon was amused with her, but she knew she hadn't said anything funny. She didn't share his smile.

"A pleasure trip?"

"A *pleasure* trip?" he repeated with a wider smile. "You mean like am I going home to get pleasure?"

"I meant business or pleasure; it just came out wrong." She felt it more annoying than funny. "And of course, that would be none of my business."

"Then why did you ask?"

Taylor finally looked down at her sweatshirt to see that Mickey Mouse's whole head was missing. "Oh, no. Look what you do to me." She dropped her sponge onto a tray, grabbed a thick paper towel and swiped at Mickey. "I'm only trying to have a conversation with you."

He silently watched her dabbing at her breasts then finally added in monotone, "I'm going home to take care of business."

Catching his tone, which sounded just short of frustration, she set down the paper towel and studied his face. She'd much rather see him amused, she decided, than frustrated with her somehow. She shook her head, then said in a business-like tone. "Is business picking up for you in California? Are you getting enough work?"

His jaw dropped. "Is that what you wanted to know?"

Well, since she decided not to go back to the pleasure part, which she really wanted to talk about, she figured this was a safe topic and a better thing to ask. "Yes."

He raked a hand through his hair, sighed, then headed for the door. Sarcastically he said, "Should be enough work to keep the food on the table."

Dillon looked back at her, and she smiled and said, "Well, good."

He shook his head as he left the room. King followed at his heels.

"And I'm the crazy one?" she said to the empty room.

Her adrenaline was up, thanks to Dillon, so she worked a little harder and faster on the walls, mumbling to herself on several occasions. When she finished all but the cleanup, she heard a noise in the hall.

"I brought you a peanut butter sandwich. Thought that's the least I can do, young lady," said Grandpa, winded from the stairs.

"Oh, how nice. Wow. Thanks."

"Now, I can see the wheels turning in your head, Taylor, but don't think I'll be up on that roof tomorrow. I made this sandwich out of guilt, not energy."

"Well, whatever it takes." She patted his arm and took the sandwich.

"Did you make Dillon mad again? He stormed out of this house like he'd seen a ghost."

What a play on words, she thought. "I suppose I did. Sorry, Grandpa."

"You should be telling *him* you're sorry, not me."

Grandpa looked around for somewhere to sit and Taylor pulled a chair out of the hall.

"This room looks really nice, but then papering is your thing. Real nice."

Glad for the change in subject, she explained what she did to the ceiling and walls.

"Yep. Looks very nice. Why is Dillon mad?"

"Oh, I don't know. I guess I asked too many personal questions."

"Well, I guess a lot of people don't like to be questioned." He watched her closely.

"He's going home to California for a couple of days, he says. Business, or pleasure, or something," she said and stacked her brushes, sponges and other paraphernalia onto a newspaper.

"Do you know how much of the roof he has left to do?" he asked.

"No, I don't. Remember? I'm not supposed to get on the ladder."

Then, when she saw the concern on Grandpa's face, she added, "Oh, he's coming back, don't worry, Grandpa."

"I was thinking that I'd like him to do some other things for us. I have a CD, a cash dividend that I can use…and I'd like to see the blackberry bushes cleared away in the backyard."

"You know we have Calvin Sweeney for the backyard."

"Calvin Sweeney doesn't belong with us, and besides that he seems to work about as much as I do around here."

She smiled as she took a bite of the sandwich, the first evidence of Grandpa's work. "Well," she said with a mouth full, "I really don't want Calvin to go yet, at least not until you feel a little better. I feel safer with him here."

"I thought that's what we have King for."

"Humph. Well, let me think things over, Grandpa. Then I need to talk to Dillon. You know, maybe Jerry would help me work on the backyard."

"That's a possibility. But I think we'd both like to see Dillon helping us with a few things. When he comes back."

Grandpa stood and walked slowly to the window. "Nice view of the backyard from here. Hey, I see Jerry trying to feed King something. He shouldn't do that."

Taylor joined him at the window. Jerry looked toward their kitchen window, positioned himself so that he couldn't be seen, and gave King what looked like pieces of meat. "No, that's not good. King's confused enough about who his owners are. I'll talk to him about it."

Dillon said he had a bad feeling about Jerry, but she didn't think Jerry had anything to gain by feeding King. More likely, Jerry had some extra food and only wanted to be nice. He already demonstrated his good character by spending some of his free time with a sick old man. She expected only good things from Jerry.

AFTER THREE DAYS, GRANDPA'S WORDS CAME BACK TO HAUNT HER. Dillon hadn't returned. Taylor didn't need anyone around to make her doubt her goals and the people around her; however, the fear of not having someone fix the roof far outweighed any confusing emotions.

When Taylor arrived home from work and didn't see Dillon's pickup, her stomach began to ache. After setting her book bag on the porch, she walked to where the ladder leaned against the house. She was glad that it was still there because she didn't think she had the muscle to bring it back to standing.

If Dillon didn't return, she needed to know what was left to do on the roof, so she could make plans accordingly. A plan, she hoped, that would calm her nerves. She climbed the ladder.

It looked to her as if the roof was still at the beginning stage as he'd not quite finished pulling off the old shingles. A pointed portion of the roof, the turret room, was still left to do. Taylor knew she could never do the turret roof, not if her life depended on it, because it was scary enough just standing on the ladder.

Her eyes filled with tears. She had someone here to fix it and she'd offended him, and he'd never be back.

"Oh, Dillon, I'm sorry," she said with a sob.

She turned her head toward the sound of a vehicle, a black pickup truck pulled into the driveway. She couldn't remember anything making her so happy. She grinned down on Dillon as he left his truck and headed her way.

He frowned and she quickly realized what was wrong: She was on the ladder.

"Get down from there," his deep voice thundered.

It irked her that he'd been gone for a while, and he didn't even greet her but yelled at her instead. Forgetting her apology made only moments ago, she countered. "Oh! I forgot being on the ladder is one of the Ten Commandments."

"It's the eleventh."

She stood as frozen as a statue.

"Now would you *please* come down?" he asked with a little more composure. He stood at the bottom of the ladder, his hands on both sides to steady an already steady ladder.

Taylor followed his eyes. "Stop looking up my skirt!"

"Not much you can do about it from up there."

She let go with one hand and tried to pull the two ends of her jean skirt together between her knees.

"All right. I'll turn away. Just get both hands on the ladder."

She couldn't stay up there forever, even though she wanted to at the moment. She climbed down to the ground and put her hands on her hips. "You didn't turn away, did you?"

"Hey, I broke a commandment, you broke a commandment. What were you doing up there anyway?"

"I thought maybe you weren't coming back, and I needed to see what was left to do."

"You thought I wasn't coming back?" he asked, his voice rising.

King approached with Grandpa not far behind. "Glad to see you made it back, Dillon. I was afraid my granddaughter might have chased you off."

"Of course, I'm back. I'm a man of my word," he answered Grandpa with a smile, then flashed a scowl at Taylor.

"Listen, Dillon, could you sit down with us for a few minutes." Grandpa pointed to the house.

"Uh… Okay."

This bothered Taylor. She'd been so consumed with worrying over Dillon's absence that she hadn't thought about the possibilities of having Calvin or Jerry help her. She had yet to ask them.

Nevertheless, this old Victorian needed to be Grandpa's reason for living. As Taylor walked into the house, she realized she had what she wanted. Grandpa felt better and he had an interest in the house.

"Your health has improved in my absence, Gilby."

Taylor was glad that someone else noticed, that she wasn't only dreaming.

Grandpa held up a hand. "Yes, a little bit better. It is slow though, slow. I want to know how long you will be in the area. We have some additional work we'd like done."

Dillon let out a breath and his eyes went from Grandpa to Taylor and back again. "What do you need?"

"Let's go in here so I can sit down. I get tired so easy." Grandpa slowly led them to the kitchen. The three sat around the round table that fitted four.

"Get me some paper and a pencil, Granddaughter."

Taylor, glad for the duty, tried to compose words to say they really didn't need Dillon after he completed the roof. After all, she and Grandpa could fix everything else in good time, and with Dillon gone she wouldn't be a lunatic anymore.

Grandpa cleared his throat. "Now tell me how much time you have left in Idaho? When will you need to get back to work in California?"

"First let me hear what you need to have done."

Taylor thought he answered a little apprehensively.

"Now that it's just about spring, I'd like to see the blackberry bushes cleared away from the backyard."

"Now, Grandpa, Calvin Sweeney gets free rent to tend our yard."

"That's true," Dillon stated, the muscles in his face starting to relax.

"Calvin Sweeney spends most of his sober hours fighting King and tinkering with the rose bushes. If tinkering is what you call it."

Taylor covered her smile with a hand, then sobered. "*I* had planned to work on the bushes."

Both Dillon and Grandpa shook their heads.

"With Calvin," she added.

"Well now, Taylor, you arrive home most days around four o'clock. Is that correct?" asked Grandpa.

"Yes."

"So, about the time you get changed and ready to work I'd say Calvin would be about three sheets to the wind."

She hadn't thought of that. She rubbed her chin with the back of her hand and looked down at King who burrowed under the table to nestle up against their legs.

"Let me talk to Sweeney, first," said Dillon, the uneasy look back on his face. "What else did you want done?"

"The house needs to be painted. It's so in need of paint it looks haunted. What must the neighbors think?" Grandpa asked with a smile.

"Yes, what must the neighbors think?" Dillon asked Taylor.

Dillon opened the opportunity for her to tell Grandpa what the neighbors really thought of the place, but Taylor didn't take the bait. She smiled sweetly at Dillon and said, "I'm sure they're used to it by now."

Then looking back at Grandpa, she added, "Now I'm sure I've told you that painting the house is what I plan to do on my spring vacation."

"Of course, I remember, but how are you going to get to the really high places."

"The ladder, of course."

Both men shook their heads. Even King looked up at her and whined.

"I just caught her up on the ladder in that tight skirt," Dillon said to Grandpa, talking about her as if she wasn't even there.

Both men looked at her and shook their heads.

"I'm not a China doll. What century do we live in anyway?

Women do lots of things this day and age. Give me a chance, you guys."

Grandpa patted her hand, then said, "And you are a darned good teacher, Taylor. Now calm down. I have a little extra money and I would like to make your, our, life a little easier."

Yet, Dillon needed to leave, to go back to California. "Maybe I could ask Jerry to help me."

Grandpa said, "Now dear, I've seen the way he looks at you and-"

"The way he looks at me?" She couldn't believe where this conversation was going. Jerry had always been proper around her, and she was about to say as much when Dillon broke in.

"Well, maybe you should see less of *Garcia* if it makes you uncomfortable." He turned to Grandpa. "For her to ask him for help would only encourage him."

"Oh, I agree," added Grandpa.

"And what about my asking you to help? Are you going to take it the wrong way?"

Grandpa answered before Dillon could respond. "*I* am the one asking for help, not you, dear."

"Yes, it is quite clear that Gilby is doing the asking."

Taylor felt her face redden. "But you have work in California, right? How is your business doing there?"

"Very well, but if I deem this important then I have others that can assist me while I'm away. Like Jeff Clark, for instance. He oversees a lot for me."

"You're Clark's boss?" Taylor asked.

Dillon nodded.

If Dillon was Jeff's boss, then why did he need to work for her, taking out bushes for goodness sake?

Taylor looked at Grandpa, waiting for his response.

"If you can take time from your busy schedule, then I would be truly honored to have you work for us," he said to Dillon.

She couldn't take this anymore. Standing quickly, she stepped on King's foot, and he let out a yelp. Undeterred, she left the room and stood on the back porch.

Taylor took in a deep breath and tried to reach some kind of calm. She looked up at the house, all the way up. After seeing how hard it would be to paint every area of the house, she groaned. She really didn't like heights. It irked her that Dillon could do everything he set his mind to do. He even knew about cohesives and wallpaper. She wanted to be moxie, but even her grandfather didn't have confidence in her abilities.

Stepping off the porch, she walked over to view what probably used to be a nice yard now covered with blackberry bushes and weeds, an old tire, and an assortment of garbage. At least this job was ground level.

She walked into it, reaching for an old, whipped cream can and her skirt caught on blackberry thorns. Trying to pull at the prickly branches scratched her leg and she learned quickly her skirt would be ruined if she yanked at it.

Reaching in at a different angle, she painfully scratched her hands. Tears came to her eyes when she realized, how helpless she was. She looked at her surroundings, no neighbor close enough to hear her cry of help. If they did, they certainly wouldn't come to this haunted domicile. She doubted Calvin was in any shape to rescue her. It would be dark soon, thus she had no choice but to think of Dillon.

He was like a knight-in-shining-armor she didn't want but needed. It was the twenty-first century; she wasn't supposed to need a man. And why, for goodness sake, couldn't he be ugly? It would be much easier for her to do business with an ugly Dillon. Okay, now she'd lost her mind.

"Help," she said half-heartedly.

Dillon probably didn't hear her, but rather came out to say

goodbye. He stood on the porch a moment until his eyes focused on Taylor.

"Could you come and help me?" she asked in a small, humble voice.

He said nothing but shook his head as he approached her, a solemn look on his face.

"Be still." He took a small cutting tool from a pouch rigged on his belt and cut away at the branches.

"You know this skirt is really not the best thing to be working in. Now I didn't mind it up the ladder, but this is a little much," Dillon said when he set her free.

Taylor almost made a snide remark but thought better of it. After all, she could've been out here all night if Grandpa dozed off. Instead, she said, "Thanks for helping me."

"Well, I'd rather do this than have to pick up the pieces after Humpty Dumpty fell off the great wall," he answered and pointed to the tallest peak of the house.

His lack of confidence in her was disconcerting. Losing control, she lashed out, "You make me crazy; do you know that?"

"You mean you're not like this all the time?" he said sardonically, then turned her around by the shoulders and bent over to inspect her injuries. "You're bleeding, but only a little bit. It must sting."

"Yes, it stings."

Dillon squatted down and began touching the area behind her knee and lower thigh while he inspected the wound. "I don't see anything stuck in it. Do you need some help medicating this?"

She hadn't heard him, she was busy wondering why in one moment he irritated her so much, and in the next moment he could physically excite her like nothing she ever imagined. Could be the hand on the thigh, she decided and reluctantly stepped away from his fingers.

"You make me crazy! Do you know that?"

Dillon sighed. "Yes, you just told me that."

She began pacing. "I want to know a few things, okay?"

"Will you believe what I say?"

"Of course," she replied. "But remember, actions speak louder than words."

He looked at her like she had a bad case of PMS.

"So, your business is booming," Taylor shot in.

Dillon's eyebrows furrowed. "Yes."

"Are you going to do this work for me? Oh, I stand corrected, Grandpa?"

"I think so."

She stopped in front of him. "And you have plenty of work to do in California?"

"Uh… Yes."

Cynically she said, "Then you're going to stay in Idaho just to cut down blackberry bushes?"

"That's one of the reasons."

"Then what else would keep you here?" Taylor asked, her hands up in question.

This time Dillon started pacing. "And do you expect me to give an account to you for everything I do?"

Taylor didn't answer. The cool evening air caused her to cross her arms, but she wasn't going in yet. Not until she had a few more answers. She watched Dillon reach down and pick up the whip cream can, effortlessly retrieving it.

"There couldn't be a thing you would want from Grandpa."

"Not a thing."

"What could you possibly want from me?"

Dillon looked down at her legs and chuckled softly. "Now don't take me wrong, I wouldn't cut down blackberry bushes with just any woman."

"You know what I think?"

"I never know what you're thinking."

"I think that you'd just cut down one bush with me and then you'd be gone in the morning. And I'm not a one bush kind of girl."

Dillon stood straighter and crossed his arms. "Now let me tell you what I think. I think I anger and excite you all in one breath and you're afraid of that, so you want me gone."

She turned away from him. "I'm not afraid of you," she said, lacking the energy in her voice to try and prove it.

He shook his head. "If you would have remembered something I told you at the beginning, that I had other business here in Trillium Falls, then we probably wouldn't be having this conversation. Besides I'm doing you a favor, you know as well as I do it's like pulling teeth to get someone out here to fix your roof.

"Things are tough out in the real world, Taylor, business is survival of the fittest. I think you are probably a great first grade teacher, but I'm not convinced your talents lie in reconstruction."

Taylor grew weary of hearing how she fell short this evening, first by Grandpa and then by Dillon.

"Come closer and I'll show you what I'm talking about when I say you fear me," Dillon said.

Cautiously she walked over, not knowing what Dillon had in mind. Her heart picked up a beat when he slowly gave her a hug, running his hands through her long hair. When he released her, he tenderly cupped her chin with a hand and gave her a soft kiss that touched her heart. He put his arms around her again and parted her lips with his tongue, kissing her until she melted into him, and her legs weakened. Finally, he broke the chain of kisses and looked down at her.

"This is not fear," she said in a confused daze.

"No, this is lust. The fear sets in when I leave."

As Dillon turned to leave, he said, "I know because I feel it, too."

Taylor watched him go, took a deep breath to steady herself, and considered his words. She'd have to admit she did have fears. How could she take such an emotional risk with her world as tumultuous as it was? She believed there would come a time when the insanity of being drawn to such a needy woman would override his attraction for her. In that case he'd be gone as fast as the speed of sound.

Even if she gave in to her passions and he turned out to be the perfect Mr. Right, his home is in California. A long-distance relationship was extremely hard to do.

Sure, she had her fears. Besides the workload, what could he possibly fear about her? She had a logical, sensible, and stable side to her. The problem was he'd just not seen it yet.

———

If Taylor was not mistaken, Dillon had lost some weight. It didn't surprise her since the roof required a lot of hard physical labor. Because of the condition of the roof, he'd had to strip off the old shingles and put on plywood before he could attach new shingles.

Through her car windshield she watched him put together two sawhorses, then stack plywood beside it on the ground. If she could just figure out how to help him, it would make his task a little easier and he would be able to leave them sooner than planned.

Besides that, she needed to learn to be able to handle any tool if she planned to live here for any length of time. She didn't want to just watch Grandpa restore the place, she wanted to help him, too.

"I need...no, I want to help you," she said, and dropped her book bag on a porch step.

Dillon looked at her suspiciously, as if waiting for the other shoe to drop.

Taylor went over and stood before him, watching him stick a flat, carpenter's pencil behind his ear. "What can I do?"

"Nothing."

"No, really, there's got to be something I can do."

His lips thinned and she spotted dark circles under his eyes. "Please."

DILLON SEARCHED TAYLOR'S FACE AND SAW NOTHING BUT earnestness there. A simple offer to help. It would have been easier for him to deny her if she'd been irritated with him as usual, or pushy. But after their last conversation, he knew that she only wanted to work on her house, and no one seemed to take her serious. No wonder she was irritated. He was the guiltiest, because ever since he'd laid eyes on her, he wanted her to need him. He still wanted her safe and would make sure she was, as long as he was around.

Her chin moved up, so he could see her determination. Of course, he'd say yes to this face, this woman, and it down right scared him to think she had the power to make him want to please her. After his last girlfriend, he thought the single life was just fine until he met this woman.

He searched her face for another moment and said, "Okay, I can use some help. Go get changed out of your good clothes. But try to make it snappy, I only have so much daylight."

In record time, Taylor made it back to the worksite.

"THESE ARE SAWHORSES," HE TOLD HER.

Taylor bit her tongue so she wouldn't say, "Duh." She planned to be all business, so nodded her head.

"I need to cut holes in these sheets of plywood for the vents." He grabbed one off the ground and set it across the sawhorses.

"Next you take a framing square, and put it like so, and mark the size of the cut we need to make."

Taylor wondered if it was wise to start her do-it-yourself career with a power saw. Determination won over. "Okay."

"Stand right here." She did and he stood behind her, trapping her between the plywood and his hard body. Hand over hand he guided her as they cut along the lines with the skill saw to make a vent hole.

When the wind blew against them, Dillon smelled like a mixture of sheets hanging on the line to dry, and a faint scent of aftershave. Part of her wanted to melt against him and swoon, to forget her problems and get lost in him. Taylor closed her eyes then opened them, when the practical side of her won out, and watched and listened intensely as Dillon worked.

She smiled. "Are we done?" she asked.

"No, we're just getting started, Taylor. Are you really serious about this?"

"Yes, yes. Let me try one."

Dillon demonstrated how to maneuver the plywood onto the sawhorses. After he grabbed a thick rubber band from a toolbox, he twisted her hair into a ponytail. She did the measuring, stuck the pencil behind her ear and cut the next vent hole with little guidance from Dillon. Proud, she smiled brightly.

"That's my girl. Now if you can keep cutting these I can do more above." When she nodded, he kissed the top of her head and moved toward the ladder. She let herself savor the kiss for a moment, then started back to work.

CHAPTER 8

*T*aylor didn't make many friends at school, but to all appearances students and staff alike seemed to forget she lived in a haunted house. Still, she doubted the Christmas staff party would be held at her home.

At school, she could forget that Grandpa wasn't well, and put her needy old, dilapidated house to the back of her mind. And here on most days, she thoroughly enjoyed teaching young minds.

One morning, Taylor arrived early to work on a new unit about birds. She was nearly halfway done by eight AM when the intercom sounded. "Quick teacher's meeting in the library. Everyone be there," the principal said firmly.

She glanced at her calendar, thinking she merely forgot, but didn't find a notation about a teacher's meeting. Grudgingly, she left for the library.

Johnna motioned for Taylor to take the seat next to her. "Did you know about this meeting?" she asked Johnna.

"No, it's unplanned. Something's come up, I guess. Probably going to get scolded over not contributing to the coffee fund,"

Johnna said with a twinkle in her eye, then grew serious. "How's your house coming along?"

"Well, I got one room finished and I have a guy working on my roof. I think he's going to do some other stuff, too."

"I thought people around here are afraid to work for you," Johnna whispered, as the meeting was called to order.

"He's from California," was all Taylor had a chance to say.

John Starr always appeared businesslike in a suit and tie, and never succumbed to casual Fridays. She wondered if perhaps it was to gain respect from the students. They respected him, but she suspected it had more to do with the fact that he shaved his head and the students thought it was cool.

"We've got some good news and some bad news. Which do you want to hear first?" After some grumbling, John continued, "As you know the bond measure failed again. That means we are going to have to put our heads together and try to make some decisions about the budget next year.

"There is a student number increase. As it is we don't have space for another classroom and with cuts, we may even lose a teacher or two."

Taylor did know student numbers increased, so she thought she'd be needed for some time. Her heart seemed to freeze, then pound. She needed her income.

"We may have to lose some aide time. Music and PE are under analysis now, too."

Johnna patted Taylor's knee and whispered in her direction. "You're not alone. They'll probably try to stretch me out between as many schools as they can, *if* I continue to have a job."

"What's the good news?" Tom interrupted John.

John removed his suit jacket, then rubbed the back of his neck. "Well, I guess it's good news depending on how you look at it."

Again, the group groaned, and he raised a hand. "Just after the failing of the bond measure, we were notified that there is a company that is willing to donate new computers to the school along with the cost to get them Internet accessible."

"Why that's wonderful!" said the librarian. "Then the money that was intended for technology can be used elsewhere."

"What's the bad part?" Taylor heard from behind her.

"It's a California developer. He wants to build a resort at the falls. Now, everything has been done according to rule. You know that if it isn't him then it'd be someone else. We all know that this was bound to happen, the falls are picturesque to say the least. It's progress, I'm afraid."

"Really? *Really?*" came a sarcastic reply.

"Some of your jobs are on the line, I'd think that you'd consider the alternatives."

"Are there any other alternatives?" Taylor asked.

"A bake sale won't cut it. This developer, uh…Dillon Nash, wants to make the community a better place. He says that children and our schools are our best commodity. He also said there may be other ways he can help, too. I think we should carefully consider his options."

When the meeting was over, Johnna stood up and looked down at Taylor. "Don't look so downhearted. Everyone around here knew that it was only a matter of time before developers moved in. I suppose your realtor should have told you that, too."

"No, I heard the rumor. It's just that Dillon Nash is the guy who's fixing my roof."

"What? The man buying the school computers is doing your roof?"

"Exactly," Taylor mumbled, only half there.

"What?" Johnna said again. "Gosh, that doesn't make sense. He'd have someone else fixing your roof. There's the bell. We'll talk later."

. . .

TAYLOR TOOK THE LONG ROUTE HOME THROUGH TOWN. MAIN Street in Trillium Falls, consisted of a hardware store, drug store, bakery, beauty shop, a boutique, and a title company. At the other end stood the real estate office and a small grocery store. All buildings had an old west motif or theme. The town also made a little money on tourism, with the beautiful Trillium Falls just south of town. She shook her head and thought what a shame it will be to change this quiet little town of 565 people. She knew the quaint little town would change someday, she just didn't think it would be so soon, and her knight-in-shining-armor had everything to do with it. At the same time, Dillon planned to do something good for the community. That said something positive about him, she supposed.

Obviously, she'd wondered many times why a person living in California would work in Trillium Falls. Okay, she knew he had other jobs to keep him here for a while. He was Jeff's boss, albeit, but she had no clue that he'd be affluent enough to build a resort in town. This news, consequently, made him too successful to spend time on her roof. Johnna was right, he'd have someone else up there.

Taylor wondered if there could be a possibility that his work for her had something to do with the house, however, she couldn't understand what value the house could still hold for him.

DILLON WAS ABOUT TO CLIMB UP THE LADDER WHEN TAYLOR arrived home from school. As he turned toward her, he took a moment to ponder what she would say to him.

Taylor was tired of being surprised. It was like walking through a mystery house with a surprise at every corner. Perhaps surprised wasn't the right word. Her surprise had turned to fear and then settled to irritation. Irritation led to anger.

She knew she had to tread lightly, because right or wrong, she had to get her roof finished. She sighed, thinking of motivating factors in her life, as well.

He walked over to her car, smiled, and gave her a wink that caused her heart to flutter. She sucked in a quick breath and then wondered at his ease at getting her off kilter. He smiled again as if hearing her thoughts.

Taylor mentally told herself to get a grip. "I was at school," she stated and pushed an errant strand of hair behind her ear.

"I KNOW. YOU WORK THERE." DILLON LAID A TOOL IN THE BED OF HIS truck and turned back around to face her. His smile quickly faded when his eyes settled on Taylor's crossed arms and furrowed brow.

He knew what was coming. It was only a matter of time before Taylor learned about his real business in Trillium Falls. He'd hoped she'd be pleased at this industrious side of his personality and dreamed of seeing her light up when she found out about all he'd achieved. Well, darned if he'd let her tear him down, when he'd worked so hard.

Perhaps this is what he had to learn, that she wasn't the right girl for him after all. Yet, he was frustrated because he wanted her to be, however scary committing to a woman might be for him.

"I ATTENDED A TEACHER'S MEETING TODAY," TAYLOR SAID.

When she said nothing further, he frowned and said, "Good to hear teachers meet. Listen, I'm a busy man, I've got work to do."

"Is that all you have to say?"

He turned to go back to the ladder, then pivoted. "No. Stay off the ladder, I don't have time to have sex with you today and *Garcia* is in the house." He'd moved toward the ladder, clearly dismissing her.

"Ooh! That's not funny!" In her frustration her book bag dropped to the ground.

He turned back. "What do you really want, Taylor? I don't have the time or the energy to argue with you tonight."

"Okay, okay," she lifted her hand and lowered her voice. "I was at a teacher's meeting this morning and I was told that you are planning to buy computers for the school."

"Yes, that's true."

"Were you keeping that a secret from me?"

"Listen. Gilby told me that you're a first-year teacher. So, I would think you'd be thankful for the chance to keep your job. My business move helps save your position."

"You did this for me? Humph. I'd have to think that the world revolves around me to think that's the reason."

"You're welcome. By the way, Calvin said he won't be able to help you with the blackberry bushes. Said his back's out." He left her standing with her mouth open.

That meant it would be left for him to do. She picked up her book bag, brushed it off and headed for the house.

"Maybe Jerry will be a good neighbor and help me instead," she said to herself as took the porch steps. She faked a big smile while entering the house.

"Gilby's whipping the pants off me, Taylor," said Jerry. "I think he's feeling a lot better. No finer chess opponent than this guy."

"I am feeling better," he said and nodded to Taylor, then made a chess move.

Taylor smiled, then sat down across from them, book bag in her lap. While she watched her grandfather, her heart lightened. He smiled more often. She thought he buried his smile with Grandma, but it came back. He only brought her grandmother up in conversation a few times since they moved into this house and that was to say he missed her. Presently he talked about his future with Taylor, not his past with Grandma. She wanted to jump for joy, pleased with Jerry for helping him smile today.

"When do you think Dillon will be done with the roof?" Jerry asked Taylor.

"Soon, I think. Not sure when," she answered.

Jerry rubbed his goatee. "I heard it's hard to get roofing help."

She wondered who told him that, it certainly wasn't Grandpa.

"Dillon was willing," she said, hesitantly.

"He was the guy who owned it last, right?"

"Yes."

"Seems odd he'd stay around just to fix the roof."

"He likes the pretty blonde that lives here," shot in Grandpa.

"Right, Grandpa, that's why we argue every two minutes."

"Isn't he the developer who's putting up the resort at the falls?"

"Yes."

Grandpa looked at Taylor. "Oh, really?"

"Then why is he fixing your roof?" asked Jerry before she could respond to Grandpa.

"Because of the pretty blonde that lives here," said Grandpa, firmly closing the subject. "Dillon fixed the door to the tower room. You might want to take a look at it, Taylor."

She climbed the stairs and headed toward the door. Two things struck her immediately. One, the door needed to be refinished to match the shiny handle and two, Dillon hadn't put a lock on the door.

Taylor wasted no time getting to Dillon. It started to rain, and he pulled his rain slicker on. "You didn't put a lock on the door."

He tipped his head to the side, then said, "Gilby couldn't see any reason to have a lock because there's no bathroom or bedroom up there."

Her sin of omission came back to haunt her. She still neglected to tell Grandpa the house was reportedly haunted and obviously Dillon hadn't told him either.

"Do you want a lock? Are you afraid of the room?" he asked.

She tried to sound confident, "No. No, I think the problem with this house is in other people's minds. Don't you think that's true? I mean, you lived here once."

"Can't help you there. I didn't live here," he answered and turned back to work.

He dismissed her again and it tugged at her heartstrings. She mentally tried to push the hurtful feelings aside and headed for her bedroom where she wondered why she felt confused and hurt. She supposed it was nigh impossible for her not to care about someone who tenderly helped when she was sick and gave her skills to become more capable in maintaining the house.

DILLON TURNED BACK TO WATCH TAYLOR WALK INTO THE HOUSE. He wished she wasn't so beautiful, and sexy, and amusing. *How does she keep making me want her?* he wondered.

Her allure blinded him to the degree that he'd climb up on a steep roof and work in the rain. He hated working in the rain. And for what? For an ungrateful woman who would be in a heap of trouble if it weren't for him.

What bothered him even more was her disapproval of his land-developing job. He worked hard over the years and had finally made it. Now he was financially able to give back, to help the area in which he'd developed, and he was damned proud of it. Obviously, Taylor hadn't considered the fact that someone else could have come in, not caring one hoot for the community. No, Taylor hadn't imagined that she only saw that he was ruining her neighborhood.

He wasn't some smitten teenage boy; he was a grown man who wanted to be appreciated. He'd finish the work he set out to do for them, then he would be gone, and Taylor could fend for herself. He could do that if he'd only distance himself from her. The less of her in his cross hairs the better.

TAYLOR WASHED HER FACE THEN RETURNED TO THE TOWER ROOM door. No lock. Could she deal with that? She said a brief prayer before entering. It was dark enough inside that she hand-guided her way to the switch. When she flipped the switch, nothing happened, meaning a missing or burnt-out bulb.

She'd get King to come with her and look it over first. Right now, Grandpa would be hungry, and she needed to fix dinner. She shut the door quickly and took a steadying breath.

Jerry didn't stay for dinner. By the time she thought it would be a nice gesture to invite Dillon, he was gone.

While eating, Grandpa resolved to put new electrical outlet covers on the walls in Taylor's room. He decided if he got tired, he could sit on a stool and do it. He thought of many things he could do around the house that way. After dinner, he asked Taylor to fetch the stool before she started the dishes.

Taylor grinned, again feeling some of her worries lift for the first time since Grandpa fell ill. He ate better and his sleeping patterns normalized. Until now, she began to think he was no longer interested in renovation. She knew in short order she would be helping him reconstruct this house.

The next thing she heard was a series of thumps and one final boom. Her heart thundered as she ran to the foot of the stairs to discover Grandpa bruised, battered and unconscious.

"Grandpa. Grandpa!" She couldn't rouse him. King bounded in and licked his face. Taylor grabbed him by the collar and pushed him outside.

Her hands shook. Should she move him? No, she didn't think so. She also didn't know if she could get anyone in this haunted house to help her.

Although still breathing, she feared Grandpa might die. She called 911. Waiting for the ambulance was torture.

Paramedics and an ambulance both arrived. Three men stood at her door, obviously biding their time, seeing who would enter the house first.

Taylor had no patience. "If you don't get in here and take care of this man, I'm going to sue!"

They took him to the hospital for x-rays. His doctor decided he was to stay at least one night for observation. Grandpa had a concussion and an impressive array of bruises, but nothing broken.

"Grandpa? Perhaps we rushed things a bit too fast. You probably got tired and slipped."

Grandpa looked at the ceiling until the nurse left his room. "No, I wasn't tired."

"But Grandpa-"

"No. I was pushed," he said in a whisper.

She wondered if he'd hit his head too hard. Perhaps confusion was part of having a concussion.

"Don't look at me like that. I *know* I was pushed."

"But we were the only ones in the house."

"I was pushed."

He seemed sane. She slapped her hands to her face. "Did you see anyone?"

"No, I felt a hand. A strong push."

"Sh...should we call the police?" she asked.

"I don't know. I don't really want this house in the papers again."

Taylor took a step back. "You know about the house?"

"Yes, Jerry told me," he said with a wince and touched his shoulder.

Jerry lost favor in her eyes. He asked, and answered, too many questions.

"Stay here with me tonight. Get a substitute for tomorrow. I'm sure the hospital can bring in a cot and first thing in the morning we'll go home. We'll decide what to do then."

Poor King had been waiting outside the house and met her car as she drove in the driveway. After loading him up, she dropped him off at a pet motel. Thank goodness King didn't need her because she was afraid to go into her own home alone.

CHAPTER 9

Grandpa walked slowly around the living room. Taylor tried to get him to go back to bed, but he refused. He wanted to stay downstairs, dressed and on the couch. He didn't say much, but she could see the wheels turning in his head.

Taylor hardly slept the night before, wondering who pushed Grandpa down the stairs. They had nothing of real value to interest a burglar; however, she'd rather think the intruder a burglar than the alternative, a ghost. Her hopes vanished when she went through their things and found nothing amiss.

Taylor put some leftover roast beef on a paper plate, let King have a smell, and headed for the stairs.

Grandpa looked over at her. "I thought you just ate."

"Still hungry," she lied and went up the stairs, King, hot on her trail.

She stopped at the tower room door. "Now King, I want you to go in this room and look for Casper," she whispered, then placed the plate of beef just inside the door. Stepping aside, King squeezed past her, and she shut the door behind him. She put her ear to the door, King began to whine, then bark at the door. She didn't want Grandpa to know what she was doing, so she opened the door. Having finished the roast in seconds, King came out, went down the hall and stairs to Grandpa.

"Some guard dog you turned out to be," she grumbled.

Taylor was about to get the plate when she heard another voice downstairs. After a few quick breaths, she peeked into the doorway, but it was too dark to see anything, so she shut the door and went downstairs.

"Yesterday, after you left, I was outside playing fetch with King," she heard Grandpa tell Jerry. "I threw a stick and I guess I slipped and fell right on my face. Old King thought I was playing some kind of game and laid right down beside me."

Taylor looked down at King and he yawned in response.

Jerry glanced from Grandpa to Taylor. "Oh?"

Not knowing what to say, Taylor only nodded.

"Well, somebody has to exercise King and obviously you weren't going to do it," Grandpa's voice rose beautifully. So good was his acting that for a second, she almost asked if he really thought King needed more exercise.

Jerry seemed placated. He sat down next to the chessboard.

Taylor looked at Jerry through narrowed eyes. She hadn't forgiven him for telling Grandpa the house was haunted. Surely, he was smart enough to realize that Grandpa didn't know anything about the house. The sick old man didn't need ghost stories to upset him.

"Jerry, Grandpa needs to take it easy. Could you come back another time?"

Grandpa didn't comment, so Jerry followed Taylor to the back door. "We saw you feed something to King the other day and we'd appreciate it if you didn't give him any treats. We want King to be loyal to us, you know?"

"Oh, uh... Sure." His face reddened. "I had some extra restaurant food I thought he'd like."

When she didn't respond, he added, "Sorry, I understand. If there is anything I can do for you now that Gilby is under the weather again, let me know."

Now she felt like a heel. No, pitiful. She bit at her bottom lip. Maybe she'd judged him too quickly. "I'm sorry, I'm tired and grouchy."

"I know you're tired," he said softly. "Please, tell me what I can do."

Even though Jerry could be annoying, she needed him. "Do you have an evening off in the near future?"

He nodded.

"Could you stay with Grandpa? I have some errands to run-"

"Certainly," he cut in, "I don't work tomorrow night."

"Good. About five thirty, then? I'll have something ready for the two of you to eat."

"I'd appreciate that." He nodded and left, with King following. Through the window, she saw him pick up a stick and throw it for King. King didn't respond and Jerry looked back toward the kitchen. Taylor stepped away before he saw her.

Grandpa cleared his throat and Taylor turned toward him. "Jerry told me that he went to that new resort in town and came across one of Dillon's employees. The construction worker told him Dillon is quite successful, but not perfect. Seems he has a record. Didn't tell him what he'd done to deserve it."

Taylor's stomach plummeted and she rubbed her arms.

"Don't worry about it, we've got enough to worry about as it is. I think Dillon is a good man. He probably did something stupid in his youth, is all."

TAYLOR TOOK CALVIN SOME CHICKEN SOUP TO BE A GOOD NEIGHBOR, as well as to find out if he'd heard or seen anything out of the ordinary last night.

Calvin opened the door. "Oh, you shouldn't have, but I'm glad you did." He walked ahead of her, a hand on his hip as he limped. "How's your grandfather feeling these days?" he asked.

"Well, he took a fall last night so he's a little shaken today."

He looked away from her and rubbed his arms. Suddenly he fixed his eyes back on her. "Where did he fall? You haven't been in the tower room, have you?"

"You told me not to go in there, remember? So of course not." She felt she had to placate him. Yet, she told the truth, she hadn't made it in all the way.

"Then how did Mr. Glenn fall?" he asked skeptically.

"Now, his name is Gilby, and you should make an attempt to visit him and get to know him."

His fingers fidgeted, probably from guilt. "Well, I didn't want to bother him, his being sick and all."

"Grandpa said he was playing fetch with King, and he slipped and fell on his face." She thought she might as well stick to the same story. "Were you home last night?"

"Yes, I was here. I was trying to deaden my back pain with some vodka, I'm afraid. I don't do well with pain."

He deadened more than his back pain if he failed to hear the noise next door and the ambulance. She decided to end the questioning as he apparently missed everything that happened that night. "I'd better go. Hope your back is better soon."

"Yes, ma'am."

———

Taylor worried about Grandpa the day she went back to school. Thankfully, he was fine physically, but the mental image of him in a heap at the foot of the stairs troubled her. It could happen again, and she wouldn't be there to help him.

When she got home, she changed from a jumper to a pair of

jeans and got busy putting something together for Grandpa and Jerry to eat.

Each day after finishing work, Dillon contacted them. He didn't come to the door last night and now it was dusk, and she hadn't seen him. She tried to tell herself it was okay because she didn't want to explain Grandpa's bruises. Yet, why was he avoiding them just now?

Taylor had so many questions she wanted to ask Dillon. Why did he continue to get up on her roof day after day? It had to be one of the hardest houses to roof, and except for her small amount of help, he kept coming back to do it alone. Where did he get his money, and did he really have a criminal record? Was he a crook and could he have had something to do with Grandpa's fall?

Perhaps she was crazy, but someone must have used the ladder to enter the house on an upper floor. Dillon could have parked down the street and made it back and up the ladder without Taylor's knowledge. The neighborhood was used to seeing Dillon on the roof, they would have thought nothing of it.

Jerry came in and Taylor explained the dinner routine while Grandpa waited next to the chessboard.

Darkness had fallen and Dillon would be leaving soon. She grabbed her purse and secretly posted herself beside a front window. Dillon rubbed a shoulder with one hand and grimaced. He glanced at the front door a few times, then put his tools in the back of his truck.

After he pulled out of the driveway, she jumped in her car, staying back far enough that he wouldn't see her.

He stopped at the hardware store. A truck honked at her, so she pulled over to the side of the road. Twenty minutes, she waited.

Next, he entered the grocery store and she waited fifteen minutes more.

When he stopped to enter the drug store, she sighed heavily at the thought of spending her whole evening in a parking lot, however, he came out shortly.

Finally, he pulled into an old motel at the edge of town. She slowed down and waited for a few minutes before parking across from the parking lot.

Dillon stood in the doorjamb, arms crossed, looking at her across the way. He suddenly stepped in front of her car and hand signaled for her to come out.

"What are you doing?" he asked.

TAYLOR GRIPPED THE STEERING WHEEL AS IF TO HOLD HERSELF BACK. "I'm trying to find out where you live."

"I suppose it would've been easier to have asked me, but then you haven't spoken to me in two days."

"Easier? Hey, wait a minute, *I* haven't spoken to you? *You* haven't spoken to me." Taylor pointed her finger at him. Dillon grabbed her finger, then wrist, and led her up out of the car and toward his room.

At the door, his heart beat like a lucky teenage boy taking his prom date to a motel to finish the night. To calm himself, he took a deep breath and let it out slowly. He wasn't supposed to think that way anymore. He took another breath.

"Well, this is it. Not much, but the best old Trillium Falls has to offer so far."

INSIDE, TAYLOR GLANCED AROUND LOOKING FOR ANYTHING irregular. From the doorway, she could see the room had a kitchenette, two queen beds and a bathroom. The bed was made and the carpet, albeit old, was vacuumed around different piles of clothes and an overstuffed tool bag. His laptop computer sat on the edge of his bed, along with a couple of paper grocery bags. Besides what was on his computer, she'd learn nothing about him from this room.

"I'm shutting the door," he said and reached around her. "I'm cold."

"But shouldn't we keep it open?" She waved her hand toward the parking lot. "It's a small town and all."

Dillon shut the door. "No." He took the paper bags and proceeded to pull out the contents. "You hungry? I'm putting some burritos together."

Taylor twisted her hands until she realized what she was doing. "No, thank you." She sat down next to the computer and stared at the closed cover.

"What are you looking at?" he asked.

"I think you can learn a lot about a man from his computer." She put a hand on the top.

"I'd rather you ask me a few questions instead. I don't want you deleting, or downloading, or anything you might accidentally do."

"Understandable." She stood up and crossed her arms. Okay, she needed a reason for being here. "Well, maybe I am getting a little hungry. What's in the other bag?"

"Since you continued to follow me after my first two stops, I stopped at the drug store and bought condoms."

TAYLOR'S FACE REDDENED AND HER JAW DROPPED. WELL, SHE SHOULD think twice before following a man around town and then coming to his room. Not safe. He gave her a minute to process the information and then tossed her the bag.

With an automatic reflex, she grabbed the bag. Her mouth opened and then closed.

"You at a loss for words?" he asked.

She laughed nervously. "Why would you think that? I mean, I didn't think you…"

"You're a beautiful woman, Taylor. You followed me. What else would I think about?"

She clutched the bag with a death grip, realizing her foolishness. He turned and crumbled raw meat into a pan.

"Empty the bag."

"I...I - "

"Just empty the bag."

He focused on her face, as a package of razor blades and a pack of mini breath mints hit the counter.

"Very funny," she said. "Is this all?"

"Hey, those blades are good but expensive." Dillon looked for signs of relief, but instead saw a variety of emotions cross her face before she laughed.

"I want you to think twice before you follow some man you hardly know to a motel."

"I didn't mean for you to know I was following you. First of all, I was trying to find out where you lived."

"I'm truly surprised, Taylor." He almost cracked a smile. When she didn't respond he opened a jar of salsa, turned the burner down and then stood before her.

TAYLOR DIDN'T KNOW WHAT TO SAY AFTER DILLON GAVE HER A mind-emptying smile. He moved closer to her, and their eyes connected for a moment or two. He took a handful of her hair and sifted his fingers through it, and she tensed, wondering what he had done to get a criminal record.

She nearly jumped when the stove's timer went off. Dillon turned off the timer and pushed the pan to the back burner.

Taylor sat down on the edge of the bed and put a hand across her face. A newfound sanity caused her to wonder why in the world she was here in the first place. For all she knew, he could be the one that tried to push her only living relative to his death.

She watched him pull flour tortillas from its plastic container.

"I came over here to find out why Grandpa was pushed down the stairs," she dared to say.

He turned back to her. "What did you say?"

"I said Grandpa was pushed down the stairs. Two days ago." Taylor searched Dillon's face, looking for any indication that he might know something about this. He closed his hands inward, and his eyes shot to his feet. After a moment, he pawed at his hair and pulled at his collar.

"Is he going to be okay?" he asked.

"Yes. Bumps and bruises but that's it."

"And I didn't even come in and see him the last two days."

She relaxed a little knowing that could explain his look of guilt.

"Grandpa said he was pushed. It was the same night the lock came off the tower room door."

"Did you call the police?"

"No," she replied.

"Good."

She took a step back, not sure what that meant.

"Where is Gilby? He's not home alone is he?" Dillon looked up from rolling a burrito, eyebrows furrowed.

"No. Jerry's with him."

Dillon took a bite of burrito and said out of a corner of his mouth, "Oh, that's great. Got the Grateful Dead head looking out for things. I can't believe you trust that guy. Here, do you want a burrito?"

"Thanks, no. I don't feel very hungry after all." She chewed on her lip, then said, "Jerry told me you have a criminal record."

He swallowed and set what was left of the burrito back on his plate. "Who told him?" he asked slowly and firmly.

"He heard it from one of your employees. Uh...at the resort. I don't think Jerry knows who the man is. Perhaps it doesn't matter."

"It doesn't matter?" his voice rose in anger. "I have big business in this town, and it doesn't matter? I give a man a job and he is stabbing me in the back by bringing this matter up. I'd say it matters a lot."

He looked toward his computer now, a frown on his face and wheels turning in his mind. His anger didn't concern her as much as the fact that he didn't deny any wrongdoing. She wondered what kind of crime he committed that could destroy his career in this town and it frightened her.

Taylor put a hand on her stomach. Jerry may have a big mouth, but there seemed to be a reason for that: He warned them so they'd be careful.

"You need to stay away from Jerry," he said finally.

"Jerry is my business."

"Well, I'm making him mine. I'm moving in with you. Damn that house. It's like some voodoo curse was put on all the owners."

"You're scaring me." She didn't know which part scared her the most, Dillon living with her or the voodoo curse.

He set his plate on the counter and pushed her to the door. "You need to get going, I've got things to do."

She found herself standing outside alone.

CHAPTER 10

*D*illon padlocked his tools in the shed, and brought in a couple of boxes, suitcase, and computer. He moved into the bedroom next to Grandpa's.

Grandpa had been staring at her, probably because she stood wringing her hands. "Taylor? Don't you think it's nice that Dillon's trying to help us? He must care about us a lot."

Taylor took a seat next to Grandpa on the couch. "Yes, that's nice." She patted his knee, instead of telling him what she really thought.

Dillon came back through the house. "I'm afraid I'm going to need towels and bedding. If it's a problem I can try to find some in town. Oh, and I'll chip in on the grocery bill."

"No. No. We have plenty," Grandpa shot in, forgetting the fact that *she* would be the one doing the extra laundry and cooking. She glanced up at the ceiling and reminded herself that his presence here was for their protection and well worth any effort on her behalf. She hoped.

"Taylor, are you listening?" asked Dillon.

This time Grandpa patted her knee. "I think Taylor's had a busy day. She's probably tired, right dear?"

She nodded.

Dillon rubbed the back of his neck. "I said that if you have any errands or anything I can do when I'm out during the day, let me know."

"Well, there is one thing. I've wanted to make a trip to the county office to see who originally owned the house. I would like to have a historical plaque to put on the house with their name inscribed upon it. I need to do something positive where this house is concerned," she said, ending with a yawn.

"Sure. They may not give out that information to just anybody, but I'll try."

She yawned again and rubbed her face.

"Taylor, go to bed," Grandpa ordered. "Dillon will see that I get to bed safely."

When Taylor got to the stairs, she mimicked Grandpa all the way up to her room. Even though he was right, she hated being treated like a child. She dropped into bed as she was, not having the energy to change her clothes.

In the morning, she stripped off her clothes, donned her robe and headed for the bathroom. The door opened and Dillon, wearing a pair of worn jeans, walked out in a cloud of steam. Sprinkles of water dotted his bare shoulders and the incomparability of his arms and chest overwhelmed her.

She felt like her head had been stuffed with cotton, and her open staring and blinking probably confirmed a lack of brain power. No words came, so she tried to move past him, but met him head on at every turn.

"Up on the wrong side of the bed this morning?"

"No, at least I don't think so. I'm not much of a morning person," she said.

With a hand Taylor waved him away and he let her pass. Inside the bathroom, she touched a temple and closed her eyes. Each day seemed to bring on extra challenges. She had to rise above this somehow. Find a way to gain her life back.

After a curt nod to the mirror, Taylor made a decision. Before it got dark, she'd ask Dillon to go into the tower room with her so she wouldn't have to scope it out alone. Perhaps she'd learn something important there.

———

AFTER WORK, TAYLOR STOPPED TO GET SOME INGREDIENTS FOR dinner. She had plans for the evening and little time to cook, so she decided on tacos and fresh fruit.

Dillon was up on the roof as expected and she waved before entering the house. Grandpa, obviously waiting, stood just inside the front door.

"Taylor, did you board up that broken window in the tower room?"

"No, but that's one of the first things we need to do. I can do that. I should be okay with a board, a hammer and some nails."

When he frowned, she said, "Come on, Grandpa. Of course I can hammer a board."

"No, it's already been done." Grandpa still looked concerned. Maybe he wasn't feeling good.

"Well, that was nice of Dillon. One less job to do. Hey, are you feeling okay?"

"Dillon didn't do it. You didn't do it and I didn't do it. So, who did it?"

Taylor smiled. No doubt Dillon did it, trying to scare them out of the tower room. "Why Casper, of course. Don't worry, I'll talk to Dillon about it."

Grandpa, done grumbling, settled in quietly to watch an all-day news channel, his new best friend since falling ill.

Taylor spotted Dillon's computer on the dining table and walked by it, slowly. After emptying the contents of her grocery bag, she sat down in front of the open laptop, set in sleep mode. After listening for hammering on the roof, she scooted up closer.

Her heart started pounding. She knew she was flirting with danger but continued to sit there anyway. She drummed her fingers on the table and bumped the computer just enough that a screen appeared. *Wow, that was an accident,* she said to herself.

He'd been working on a file called, "Investments." She tapped her fingers again, then hit the down arrow button that took her through the list.

She noticed the computers for her school. The price tag for this investment, sixty-four thousand dollars, was higher than she could ever imagine someone paying for public relations.

Scanning down the list, she found her house, the dates bought, sold, and prices listed. Counting real estate fees, he lost fifteen thousand dollars in selling. Footnote: Input, low. Output, high. *That was jargon for what?* she asked herself.

Looking back over the list, she could find no rhyme or reason for having this house. His other business properties didn't include a single residence. Besides, he seemed anxious to get back to his home in California, so she doubted he wanted to live in Trillium Falls for any length of time. Probably only long enough to get the resort going and that would be it.

Taylor gulped when she saw the financial prospectus for the Trillium Falls Resort. He invested millions of dollars into it. She couldn't see how anyone would want to borrow so much money. Talk about risk taking.

She moved back up the list and noted that the name Kirsten Olson was listed three times. A business partner, perhaps?

This business made Dillon a powerful man. Where did all the money come from? How did a young man get his hands on all this opportunity? She covered her face with both hands. Stress and unease settled around her shoulders. Something was terribly wrong with this picture.

All hammering stopped and Taylor looked at her watch, then moved from the computer as fast as she could.

"Taylor, I have something to ask, and I want you to listen carefully."

"Sure. What, Grandpa?"

"I think it's time we had a heart to heart about why you bought this house. What were you thinking?" he asked in a low voice. "I think we've been afraid of hurting each other by talking about this."

Taylor nodded. She had been dreading this conversation, a subject too hard emotionally on her to undertake. She didn't want to look back at the time she'd almost lost her grandfather and the quick decisions that followed.

He already knew about the house, nothing else she could say would upset him any more than that. Leaning back, she crossed her arms. "The doctor told me that you needed to get involved with life again, that you had to have other interests besides Grandma. Looking back, I remembered you enjoyed renovating houses."

"I did that to make extra money. Teachers don't make much you know."

"But you made some incredible changes to those houses, surely you enjoyed the work, too."

"Well, sure, but I was younger and a bit healthier, too. So, let me get this straight. You didn't buy this house because you loved it, but because it needed repairs and I needed something to live for."

Taylor was determined not to cry, and worked hard to add enthusiasm when she said, "I like this house. It can be magnificent. I would like to see it rebuilt. Then, yes, it would be the house of my dreams."

When Grandpa looked her in the eye and sadly shook his head, she turned away from him and tried to keep her voice from breaking when she added, "You're my only family and the only one left in this world who loves me. Do you think I would give up so easily on you?"

"Taylor, you want me to go on forever. I can't go on forever. You seem to forget that you will someday marry and have a family of your own. They will be your family and they will love you."

"I may never find the right guy for me, Grandpa."

"Taylor, you know how to get along with children and you know how to get along with old people. Your whole world revolves around them. But now you've got to learn how to get along with the people in-between. It's not just the men, you left your last close friend when you finished college."

"I don't need them, Grandpa, I've got you."

"You have me for a time, that's all."

Taylor's eyes filled with tears, and she sniffed. "Don't talk like that, Grandpa."

"I'm going up to take a quick rest, but before I go, is there anything else you need to tell me that you haven't already?"

"Only that King is doctor prescribed for you."

Grandpa shook his head and said sadly, "I'm too much work for you, Taylor."

DILLON WONDERED WHAT IT WAS ABOUT HIM THAT MADE WOMEN want to use him. True, up until now, Taylor may not have asked for his money, but she was needy of two things. She used him to fix things and for protection.

Taylor epitomized a living reminder of his attraction to the wrong kind of woman. He, at this moment, pounded nails into a woman's roof as testimony. It was all about what he could give a woman, not what a woman could give him.

He'd learned the hard way. His last girlfriend didn't even seem to miss him when he traveled on business if he left her a charge card. Once, when called away on short notice, he'd neglected to leave her some cash and she verbally attacked him because of it. Unfortunately, love is blind, so it took some time to get a good read on her. When the realization hit, it lambasted him emotionally, and not wanting to be hurt again garnered a deep distrust of the opposite sex.

Presently, he wondered if Taylor avoided him, playing hard to get, so that he'd give her more attention. Well, two could play that game. Once she realizes her plan won't work, what will be her next strategy? If he knew the human mind well enough, he'd say she'd try to use her body to get her needs met. However appealing her body, he couldn't risk it because he knew she'd win the game. He'd be here until doomsday fixing this damn house and then what? Then he'd still have to gather his pitiful emotions and move on looking for the good woman Taylor probably only appeared to be.

Yes, this was a game all right. Nevertheless, he was determined to be a pillar of strength from now on. No more Mr. Nice Guy. Taylor Glenn, let the games begin.

TAYLOR LOOKED OUT AT THE DARKENING SKY. IT WAS NOW FIVE o'clock and nearly dusk, so Taylor went out to call Dillon down from the roof. "Could you come in and help me with something?" she shouted, hands cupped around her mouth.

"I'm kind of busy right now," he answered, clearly annoyed.

She bit her tongue to keep sarcasm at bay. If she wanted him to do anything she had to be polite.

"Taylor, I'm almost done with the roof. I want to keep going."

He was killing himself up there and deserved to have a break even if he didn't help her. One sure way to get his attention was to climb the ladder. She figured her semi-tight skirt wouldn't hurt either. She did know how to dress for work, she decided with a grin.

"Damn it, Taylor!"

"Please. This is important to me. You've worked too hard today anyway."

"Hell. Give me a second." He continued to hammer, and she continued to perch on the ladder.

"Nice of you to put the board on the broken window," she said with a smile. He wasn't going to pull the wool over her eyes.

He stopped pounding in mid swing and looked over at her, his lips forming a straight line. "You didn't put up the board?"

"No."

"Get down, I'm coming," he said sternly.

Her immediate reaction was to think she made a mistake coming out here. They can look in the tower room any old time. She stepped onto the ground; he nearly stepped on her at the bottom.

He shook his finger at her. "No more games."

She took her own finger and pointed it upward, but when he towered over her, she said timidly, "Well, I didn't think you'd come down if I didn't come up."

"Use words, Taylor, instead of your actions. You spend far too much time dreaming up what I'm thinking, then you do weird things instead of just communicating with me."

"We can't communicate, that's why I don't ask."

"Never mind." He lifted his finger again. "But you don't need to be scaring Gilby. You put up that board but you're denying it. What kind of a foolish game is that?"

Fear sliced through her when she looked from Dillon toward the boarded window. *If Grandpa didn't do it, and Dillon didn't do it, then who did?*

"I didn't do it," she choked out. This was spooky and weird. Her heart picked up a beat and her mouth went dry. "I didn't, Dillon. I wanted you to come down and go through the tower room with me before its dark. Climbing the ladder is my only offense today."

Her mind flashed to a movie she'd seen where ghosts lived a life in the house at night, while a family lived in it during the day. To end these thoughts, she looked Dillon in the eye.

Dillon's staid countenance told her nothing. King licked her hand and sat down, drawing her attention away from Dillon.

"Why didn't King bark when this happened? Grandpa's been here all the time, so he would've heard him if he did."

"He's either not the best watch dog in the world or he's familiar with whoever it is that did it. Then again he could have used a screw gun which can be quieter than a hammer."

"Well, that would eliminate a lot of people. Only Jerry, Calvin, you, Grandpa and I have been around this house. The real estate lady hardly came in, Dillon."

"Can you blame her?" he asked, looking back up at the window. "It's getting dark. Let's go check out the tower."

Dillon didn't offer a hand to Taylor, yet she took it anyway. His other hand held a flashlight that she hoped would serve as a weapon. The first thing she noticed was a musty smell, probably because the broken window allowed rainwater to blow in.

Dillon shined his flashlight around and she stood behind him as far as his hand would permit.

Except for the basement, she had never seen so many cobwebs and dust in her life. While thinking of all the spiders that must have made them, her skin prickled.

Two matching dusty-rose colored chairs and an ottoman remained in the room, one damaged by exposure to the elements. The creaking hardwood floors were refinished, but likewise had damage under the broken window. There was nothing left to see except for a closet.

Taylor pulled her arms tightly to her chest while Dillon approached it slowly. She hoped and prayed they would not find a skeleton in it, or anyone alive either. Her hands crept up to her neck; she squinted her eyes and held her breath.

Dillon whipped the door open so fast, she nearly jumped out of her skin. Upon inspection, it was an empty standard closet, albeit small.

From an unbroken window, she could see that the view was spectacular. She looked across the town of Trillium Falls into pastureland. "This would be a great reading room. You could look up from your book and gaze out the window."

Dillon reached up to lock the windows. She looked up with a smile of thanks only to find Dillon looking at her gravely.

"If you're done with me now, I guess I'll go," he said.

"What do you mean?"

"If I've fulfilled my current obligation, which would be to check out the tower room, then may I be excused?"

Slowly she shook her head, again not understanding.

"That's all I am to you, you know. Somebody to fix this or that. Well, I'm a human being, just like you are. I have needs and wants, too."

In all seriousness she said, "As your employer, uh… maybe it's time you gave me an itemized statement. I haven't paid you anything yet and it's probably high time."

"You can't afford to pay me what I'm worth, Taylor. And this is not about money, this is about using me to get things done around here. Otherwise, or afterwards, I could jump off a bridge for all you'd care."

First Grandpa gave her a lecture and now Dillon. Maybe Grandpa was right, kids and old people are her forte. "I'm sorry, I don't know what to say."

Dillon lifted two fingers to quiet her. "I think I hear Gilby."

On leaving the tower room Taylor heard it, too.

"Taylor! Dillon!"

Grandpa was at the back porch. "He's gone."

"Who's gone?" she asked.

"King's gone. Something's not right. He never goes far from the yard. He's too worried about where we are," Grandpa said. "I know he's gone."

Taylor shook her head in denial. "He's around here somewhere, I'm sure." She couldn't bear the thought of King never coming back. Suddenly all her swirling, devastating emotions expanded her chest and she could do nothing but put her mouth into her elbow and cry.

Dillon cut between them.

"What are you doing, Dillon?" Taylor asked, now dispirited.

"I'm going to go look for him."

Taylor and Grandpa followed behind.

Dillon put a hand out to stop them. "I'll go look. You wait here," was all he said before backing out of the driveway.

It took Taylor quite a while to get to sleep that night. Dillon hadn't returned with King and her thoughts went from thinking that King wasn't really gone, to how lonely and quiet the house was, and much more frightening than when King was here. True, she knew he was not a great guard dog but his presence, his being a German shepherd, made her feel safe. Even though she only had him for a short while, she knew she would miss him sorely.

SOMEONE BURST INTO TAYLOR'S ROOM. HIGHLY STARTLED, SHE turned quickly to find Dillon and a dog. It was a German shepherd, with the same coloring as King. Seeing the likeness to her beloved King caused Taylor's eyes to fill with tears.

"Get up beautiful, it's six in the morning. Time to take the pup out to pee." He sat on the edge of her bed. "No sign of King, I'm afraid, but the shelter is keeping an eye out for him. I know this dog can't replace King but there are lots of dogs in the world that could use this family's love. This boy is six months old. I heard somewhere that males make good guard dogs."

"Sounds like a sexist comment to me." She watched the dog roam from object to object, perhaps sniffing where King had been.

The pup licked her hand and wagged his tail. Already she was excited about this one. "What do I owe you, Dillon? I know this dog didn't come free."

"Nothing. This one's on me." Dillon rubbed his chin. He looked at the dog, but she surmised his thoughts were elsewhere. He probably missed King, too, she decided.

"What do you think happened to King?"

"He could turn up, I suppose. But I think someone took him."

Taylor felt her throat constrict. She felt deeply saddened and then came tears of outrage. "How could anyone take King? Why? What kind of person would do this? He was just my dog, for goodness sake."

Dillon didn't reply, he only shrugged his shoulders. The pup returned to him, and he patted his head.

"What is it with this house? If someone wants me out of here then deal with me not my dog," she said with a sniff, then her eyes widened. "Oh, but what about this dog? Somebody might try to take him, too. Did you think about that, Dillon?"

"Yes, but we'll keep a better eye on this one. He can be with one of us all the time, okay? You need a dog around here for more reasons than one."

Dillon and her new dog left the room. Dillon's thoughtfulness made her teary eyed, then she turned over and cried into her pillow, missing her beloved King.

CHAPTER 11

*I*t troubled Taylor that Dillon believed she took advantage of him. Somehow, she thought a paycheck for his services would solve everything, that if you pay someone then you are not using them. If she weren't so dysfunctional when it came to him, she'd be able to tell him that and ask him why she was his employer in the first place. However, part of her feared the unknown so much that she remained mute. Even after questioning Dillon's involvement with the house and Grandpa's fall, she had to believe she was safe with him around.

Dillon finished the roof and once the rain died down, they planned to clear blackberry bushes. She doubted he'd stay longer than that.

He made his business calls at the dining table, so it was easy for all to hear. His behavior was trustworthy, beyond reproach. From all appearances he was present only to watch out for her and Grandpa. Yet, there was nothing extraordinary about Grandpa or herself, and one could volunteer for much more rewarding missions.

Grandpa said that Dillon was around because of her, a pretty blonde. On the other hand, he kept his distance these last two weeks, spending more time with Grandpa and the puppy. It didn't make her feel pretty to be ignored like that, only jealous.

Taylor took this opportunity to spend some time on the third-floor bathroom. The old-fashioned pink tile had to go, and she took a sledge hammer to it. The exercise felt good, but what felt even better was the plans for the room that popped into her head as she worked.

———

THE DREADED DAY FINALLY ARRIVED, AND DILLON AND TAYLOR SET out to attack the blackberry bushes. When she made her way to the backdoor, she saw an array of garden tools from rakes and hoes to various types of pruners.

Dillon turned to her when the backdoor swung open. She'd been watching him try to teach the new pup to fetch a stick. He looked her up and down, then frowned.

"What's the matter? I'm not wearing a skirt. My skirts are for ladders."

He smiled. "You are dressed fine, but why don't you put this jean jacket on to protect your shirt and arms. These bushes can be nasty."

"Oh, okay. Thanks." The jacket smelled like lime aftershave, a distraction she didn't need, she realized, when she missed what Dillon said. She looked up at him in question.

"I said, you are going to need your gloves," he said slowly, carefully pronouncing each word.

"I'll be right back." Taylor headed back into the house, searching for Grandpa. She should have told Dillon that she didn't have any gloves, but she'd just as soon wear the Playtex gloves she used to wash the dishes rather than tell him she wasn't prepared.

"Grandpa, do you have some garden gloves I can use?"

"Well, I did. Look out in the shed, probably on the lower shelf by the door."

She whipped past Dillon and entered the shed, luckily finding the gloves first thing. The pup nearly knocked her down, excited by her scurrying about.

While Taylor wanted to help refurbish the house, she didn't look forward to this job. When she looked out over the yard at the thorny branches, she recalled her last tangle with the bushes and the bloody welts left on her legs. They reminded her of hundreds of barbed whips reaching out in many directions. She sighed and said, "Can't we just poison this or something?"

Dillon grabbed a lopper. "The experts say that poisoning the bushes would be great. In the fall. That way it would work through the fall and winter. But its early spring now, so let's get chopping."

After looking around at the various tools, she picked up a hoe, moved away from Dillon, and started hacking at the bushes.

She could tell he didn't know who to rescue first, the pup who got in his way, or herself, standing as if at the edge of a huge precipice grasping the hoe like a lifeline.

"Pup!" He grabbed a rope out of the shed, took one end and attached it to the pup's collar, and the other end around the bumper of his truck. The pup immediately sat down to chew on the rope. Taylor hoped that would keep him busy for a while.

"Now, Taylor, start with loppers. Trim them back first, then we'll hoe them."

"Sure, that's what I was thinking." She stood back and wiped the hair from her face with the back of her gloved hand. "I'm glad I don't have to do this every day for a living. Dealing with the behavioral problems of a six-year-old is much easier."

"Well, I don't know if that's much better. You just have to set your mind to do this."

"Oh? And how do you do that?" she asked not only interested, but to keep herself from working, too.

He handed her a lopper. "You tell yourself that if you finish the job then you get something you really want."

"You say your driving force is that you will be rewarded with your heart's desire when you finish the job, huh?"

"Well, I don't know about your heart's desire. Maybe something more practical. It could be an experience, too." He turned and gave her a wink. "What would be your reward?"

Taylor tingled all over. She always was a push over for a wink. She smiled and put her chin on her hand resting on the hoe handle. "I don't know, I guess I need to think about that one. Hmm... Chocolate, dark chocolate would be a nice treat."

"Well, whatever it is you *believe* you're going to get it. Belief will drive you. Now get to work."

He was driven all right. His muscle and force did three times the work she did.

Her voice broke their silence. "What is it you want so badly?"

"Nothing...you'd...ever...guess," he said with words driven by the force of the hoe.

Now comfort was not an option, if she shed any clothes she'd be scratched again. They worked for what seemed like hours and Taylor believed she sweat off five pounds.

Their yard debris pile was endless. "Can I burn this?" she asked, hoping for an easy clean up.

"And your experience is...?"

"Limited."

"How limited?"

"Virgin fire starter."

"That's what I thought." He pushed his hair back with a hand. "I have a plan. I'll see this through before I'm gone. I'll haul it off, have the ground tilled or dirt brought in. One or the other, don't know which just yet. Next plant grass, but you, Calvin and Gilby are on your own for the landscaping. It'll be all over at the end of this week."

If she could keep Grandpa from asking Dillon to do more work, it would be all over. They couldn't keep asking Dillon for help. He had his own life and they had theirs. It was as simple as that. At last, they could get on with their lives.

"Thanks, Dillon."

"Well, it's not done yet. Thank me later."

"Yes. And I will want an itemized bill." She turned toward the house, the day and her energy spent.

———

"YOU THINK YOU CAN PAINT THIS HOUSE ALL BY YOURSELF?" Grandpa's asked, his voice rising.

"Just calm down a bit and listen. Like I said, I have the whole week off, plus two weekends. That's nine whole days. Think of all I can accomplish in that time."

"You know darn well it's not the time factor, it's getting to all the high points of the house."

Closing her eyes, she rubbed her temples and then began again, "I know I can paint at least two thirds of this house. Perhaps soon after you'll be able to finish - "

"Finish me off you mean. Humph. What is it about Dillon, anyway? Is it the quality of his work?"

"No."

"Didn't think so. Then has he made untoward advances?"

"Uh…no."

"Maybe it's because you wanted him to, and he didn't?"

"No! We are a family of two. We need to make it by ourselves. I don't want to be dependent on Dillon."

"Well, you should have thought about that when you decided to buy this place, Missy."

The comment hurt her feelings. "I'm sorry for everything, okay? But I want us to get back to normal."

Grandpa squirmed in his seat and rubbed his knee. "All right. You do what you can do, then we'll see what problems we have when we face them." She knew he wanted to say more but guessed the tears welling in her eyes stopped him.

"Thanks, Grandpa." She kissed him on the top of his head and left the kitchen for her bedroom.

───────

THE WEEK ENDED AND DILLON, TRUE TO HIS WORD FINISHED HIS part of the backyard.

Taylor stood on the back porch watching him water the new sod.

"You've got to keep the new grass watered, Taylor."

She nodded.

He pointed. "And you probably should plant some shade loving plants in that area over there," he pointed.

"I'm sure I can find some plants that will fit."

He rubbed the back of his neck. "When you plant them, mix some fertilizer in."

"Okay."

"It would probably help your budget to plant some perennials. You know, plants that'll come back again next year. And save the receipts because they might be tax deductible if you ever decide to move."

He turned away from her now. How sad it was for her to hear his way of saying goodbye, his trying to tell her everything she needed to know to succeed before he left. If she dwelled too hard on this, it would break her heart. This had to stop ASAP.

"And look both ways before I cross the street," she added with a strained smile. Dillon returned her smile and turned toward her.

"Thanks for everything, Dillon," she said to avert her thoughts. "I'll pay your bill now."

He went to his truck, then returned with a box of chocolates and an itemized bill. First, he handed her the chocolates. "Here's what you were working for."

"Thank you," she said and turned around to write the check so he wouldn't see her eyes tear up.

Nothing further had happened in the house, so Dillon finished his work and moved out. Even though Taylor won the battle with Grandpa, she experienced a feeling of loss. The house was too quiet with Dillon gone. How could she bear to drive into the driveway and not see Dillon on the roof?

Calvin Sweeney came out of hiding the day after Dillon finished the backyard. He even talked to Grandpa about what plants they'd put around the yard.

Nevertheless, she didn't need Calvin anymore, either. Her responsibility was to Grandpa and to him only. Grandpa wanted Calvin out from day one. If he let her get rid of Dillon, then the least she could do was reciprocate.

The amount of electricity they used in one month astounded her. Even though Calvin's apartment had a separate entrance it was not set up to be anything but a maid's quarters. That meant the same address with the same water, garbage, and electric bills. For this reason alone, it could not go on. She couldn't afford to take care of Calvin, too. Especially given the amount of work he did around the place.

Thinking she heard movement outside, she went to the window and saw Calvin in the backyard. She took a deep breath and went outside.

"Hi, Calvin."

"Hello, dear."

It was four o'clock and she believed the plastic soda bottle he carried held something other than Sprite.

"I'm sorry to say this but I need you to move out." She lifted the electric bill to emphasize her next words. "I can't afford to pay all our bills and yours, too."

"But the deal was that I would take care of the grounds in exchange."

Taylor could tell by his face that this was a hard blow, but she didn't know of any other way. "That was the deal the previous owner had written, not me."

"Well...well," he said softly, more to himself than to her. "Where will I go? What will I do?"

Even though she had some ideas, she didn't feel like enabling him any further. Surely, he must have thought this out before she'd moved in. "I don't know what else to say."

He lifted his cap and rubbed his crew cut as he'd done many times before. "I guess I should start packing then."

"I'll give you a month to find another place." When he smiled, she quickly added, "And that's all."

Taylor watched him walk back to his door, shoulders slumped. Damn that real estate woman anyway, or Dillon, or whoever didn't dismiss him in the first place. Somebody left the job for the first-grade teacher; a person no one thought could make it in the business field.

Nevertheless, after Calvin went inside, she felt a load lifting from her shoulders. Now she had one less thing to worry about.

CHAPTER 12

Grandpa could barely restrain his excitement. "I've got our answer, Taylor. I researched painting supplies and found out that there's some easy scaffolding that I can put together. It's made of metal, so it's lightweight. I think we can add some of the plywood Dillon had left over from the roofing job."

"Oh, you mean so that I can reach the high parts of the house?" Her interest was piqued, not only from this grand notion but from his newfound trust in her abilities.

"Yes, I think we can do it. We can rent the stuff."

"What do you mean, we?" she asked, skeptically.

"I'm going to try and help; I've been feeling better. I can at least paint around the bottom."

Taylor bit down on her lower lip and studied him. He was doing a lot for himself these days, including helping to get dinner on the table the last few nights. She'd have to trust him on this.

A haunted house should look dark and foreboding, not light and colorful, so she chose a bright yellow color, with white trim on the wooden Victorian lace and spindle rails.

Taylor took Pup to a pet motel and then came home, and pressure washed the house while Grandpa put together the scaffolding. After the pressure wash, the house needed wire brushing and scraping.

As far as the painting itself went, Taylor decided to tackle the high spots first, thinking that if it killed her at least she wouldn't have to paint the rest of the house. Grandpa did as he planned and stuck to doing what he could reach on foot.

Taylor didn't really appreciate how large the house was until she had to paint it. Nearly every minute of her spring vacation was spent with a roller in her hand while making sure Grandpa wasn't overdoing it. It pleased her that the work he'd done hadn't fatigued him too much. She made sure he took naps and, in the evenings, he went to bed with the birds.

At the close of each day, Taylor would go out and examine their work. After only a few days, she had to admit to herself that she'd learned a valuable lesson. She discovered from the tall eves of the house, from behind a skill saw and amongst a yard full of black-berry vines, that if she could learn to master these things, she could do almost anything. She'd make it on her own.

―――――

TAYLOR PULLED INTO THE DRIVEWAY AND NOTICED THE GRASS Dillon put in was already in need of a trim. Walking into the back-yard, she spotted Calvin standing at his door with a "Sprite" in his hand. She waved a hand at him, and he nodded in return.

"Calvin, do you know if the lawnmower is in working order?"

"Don't know, Miss." He looked the other way.

Obviously, he wasn't about to volunteer his assistance. She sighed and turned to the backdoor.

"Miss?"

"Yes?" She turned back toward Calvin.

"Where's Mr. Nash?"

"He finished the work we'd asked him to do and now he's gone."

He didn't reply, only chuckled to himself.

Taylor didn't see the humor. She turned the key and entered the kitchen.

"Hi, Taylor." Grandpa's bright smile lifted her spirits. He opened a can of dog food for Pup. Pup, engrossed in the procedure, only thumped his tail when she walked by.

"Hi, Grandpa. Any calls?" Actually, she wanted to know if Dillon called to check on them but didn't say it.

"No, but Jerry stopped by."

"Really? It's been a while. Who won the chess game?" she asked while she flipped through the mail.

"He didn't stay very long. Only stopped in to say hi."

"Where's he been?"

"Well, I think he's been around. My opinion is that he was avoiding Dillon."

After tearing up a pre-approved Visa application, she turned around. "What makes you say that?"

"They both seem to be on guard when they're in the same room. Today he asked questions about him. Where did Dillon go? When will he be back? Things like that."

What was strange about that? She was on guard every time Dillon was in the room, too. "Jerry asks questions. That seems to be a pastime with him."

"Thanks for doing the dishes and starting dinner." She patted Grandpa's shoulder and left the kitchen.

"That's all I had energy for," he called out after her. "You'll have to do the dishes tonight."

"What a convenient excuse," she said with a chuckle, and then took the stairs.

At the top, she stopped abruptly as the tower room door stood ajar, the light on. She turned back and took enough stairs to reach the first landing. "Grandpa, did you go into the tower room today? Did you replace the light bulb?"

"No. I still need to pace myself a bit. Maybe I can change it later."

Her heart started to beat. With a hand on her chest, she turned back to the stairs. "Pup! Come, Pup!"

Pup, done with his meal, bounded up behind her. She led, then pushed him into the tower room, like he was a huge bodyguard. With adrenaline pumping, she followed cautiously behind. There was nothing or no one there. Pup sniffed until satisfied, then turned to look at her. After grabbing Pup's collar, she backed through the door, turned out the light and closed the door.

She told herself that the reason the light worked this time was because of faulty wiring. Yes, that would explain the reason the light was out one day and working the next, but it didn't explain who turned the light on. She mentally kicked herself for not putting a lock on the door.

Taylor washed the dinner dishes with Pup lying at her feet. She didn't have the heart to scold and move her dear bodyguard and stepped gingerly around him. She'd let Grandpa be the mean one.

Pup sat up and lifted his ears, let out a soft growl, then bounded out of the kitchen and up the stairs barking.

Moving into the living room, she could see Grandpa sitting comfortably on the couch with a book. "Must be the wind. The dog is not used to the noise the wind makes," he said to her, then turned back to his book.

Taylor was not so sure and wondered briefly if she should tell him about the door and the light. Biting her lip, she turned back toward the kitchen, and put her arms across her stomach.

Dillon was gone, he couldn't help her. Unjustified, she couldn't call the police. She couldn't tell them that Grandpa, although unstable on his feet, was pushed down the stairs. Now someone was opening the door and turning on the light in the tower room.

They would think she had as many bats in the belfry as this old house.

Turning, she stood at the kitchen doorway and looked back at Grandpa. What if he got hurt again, or killed, when she was at work? When she decided that she'd rather die than lose her only family, she went to the tower room. She found nothing except Pup sniffing around.

Perhaps Grandpa was right, she finally decided. Maybe it was the wind.

———

"You're going to be late," Grandpa said, coming in from outside with Pup.

"I know that," she snapped, frustrated. She spilled coffee on her first outfit, changed, and now she couldn't find her lesson plans.

Grandpa stepped out of the room, then came back with a file folder. "Are you looking for these?"

"Oh, yes. Thank you." She grabbed the file, her coat, bag and coffee and headed for the door.

"PMS?"

"Grandpa, you should never say that to a woman," she said, voice rising, and squeezed through the screen door.

She wished it was PMS. What she needed was a vacation and she just had one. One where she worked her fingers to the bone on a house that someone or something didn't want her to live in. In addition, she missed Dillon. At least no one bothered them with him around.

Up to this point, things happened at night. Who, she wondered, could be trying to frighten her by pushing Grandpa, turning on lights and making noises? Perhaps someone tried to scare her enough to move. Yet, besides her realtor, and staff at school, she didn't really know anyone in this town.

It couldn't be Calvin because she'd often spotted him drinking after school, and more than likely he was probably too drunk to stand up at the time of incidence.

Jerry Garcia was harmless. Maybe Dillon didn't think so, but she did. How many young men would spend any time at all with a sick old man? It was the kindness in him that made him spend time with Grandpa playing chess.

And Dillon. Why in the heck did a rich man spend all his extra time putting a roof on a house that he no longer owned? It wasn't charity because he took money for the job. Moreover, she now knew it wasn't to get physically close to her as Grandpa had voiced.

As if by magic Dillon appeared. His pickup stopped at a red light going in the opposite direction. She could barely see him through his front windshield, but she saw his hand come out of the window to greet her.

Whether guilty or not, she cared for Dillon, and seeing his familiar hand caused her eyes to tear up. The light turned green, and she had to bite her tongue to keep from crying out to him when he slowly passed by.

———

ONE DAY AT WORK, JOHNNA TOLD HER THERE'S LOTS OF documentaries telling of ghosts in old houses. Perhaps one resided there, in the tower room, she'd said. Taylor didn't know about that, but she did know that each evening when she ascended the stairs, she found the tower room door open and the light on, and each time she went inside she found nothing.

After three nights of this, she had a locksmith change the locks on the front and back doors. She told Grandpa it was because she wanted to make sure that they were the only ones with access to the house, especially after he'd fallen down the stairs. He was against it at first, but after seeing Taylor's determination, gave in.

Yet, she wasted her money because each night the door was open, the light on. Only Sunday was different, so whoever or whatever had a day of rest.

If he didn't enter by door then there must be another passage to get to the tower room. Like she'd learned from the movies, she checked all the bookcases, possible loose fireplace bricks and looked down into vents. She came up with nothing.

Maybe she did have a ghost and that was the reason someone locked the tower room door and broke the hall light out in the first place. Perhaps the spirit was even strong enough to give her grandfather a push; however, she doubted a spirit could board up a window.

Sunday night as she lay down, she prayed that the spirit was a good one. That's the last thing she remembered until Pup barked from the inside of her locked bedroom door. She sat up quickly, freezing, feeling rooted to the bed.

Something had to be happening in the tower room, but she wasn't going to go and investigate. She worried about Grandpa but knew she could only help herself now. Wanting to be invisible, she tried to make her body as small as possible. She lay awake for the rest of the night listening for noises and hearing nothing unusual.

Even though Pup's barking was loud enough to wake the dead, she found out at breakfast that Grandpa, always a deep sleeper, heard nothing.

CHAPTER 13

"And nothing happened when Dillon was living there?" Johnna asked.

Taylor exhaled. "That's correct. That makes me think that it's not a ghost."

"That's a scary thought."

"Yeah. I think Casper would be better."

"Maybe it's only teenagers goofing around."

That was something Taylor hadn't thought of. "Hey, you're giving me some hope. A call to the police will tell me if other things are happening in town, too. I'm feeling better just talking to you."

"Well, I'm glad you're feeling better because I heard that Dillon Nash is coming in sometime today with his first donation of computers."

Taylor tried not to show the array of emotions that flashed through her. "I guess you'll get to see what he looks like now."

"Yep," Johnna shot over her shoulder as she left the room.

Taylor smiled, happy with the notion that she might see Dillon again. However, there was a good chance she wouldn't even see him since she had little time away from students.

———

"Jimmy, choose which lunch you're having so we can get our lunch count in."

"Ms. Glenn?" asked Jimmy.

"Yes?"

"I forgot."

"I know you did, that's why I reminded you."

"Oh, yeah," Jimmy said with a chuckle, and stood up to get his lunch ticket.

"Ms. Glenn? I already told him that," said Jessica, arms crossed.

"Yeah, but you're not the teacher," Jimmy said with a snarl.

"I got it, Jessica," Taylor countered, ending the discussion.

Taylor stood up, then smoothed down the front of her denim jumper and tucked a pencil behind her ear. When she clipped the lunch count on the classroom door, she noticed Dillon in the hall. She put a hand on her chest while Dillon approached, wearing a long-sleeved red, button-up shirt and blue jeans.

"In the area so I thought I'd stop in and say hello."

"Ms. Glenn is that your dad?" asked Katie.

Taylor smiled thinking that Katie probably meant husband, not dad.

"No, this is Mr. Nash."

"He's her boyfriend because Ms. Glenn is not married. My mom said," Jimmy added to no one in particular.

Taylor felt her face redden. "One moment, class."

She led Dillon back to the hall leaving her classroom door open. She put her palms together, while she tried to think of what to say. Glancing back at her classroom she spotted Jimmy preparing to stand on his desk.

"Sit down, Jimmy, and get out your library book."

"I can't find my library book, Ms. Glenn," he whined.

In response, Dillon smiled at Taylor and it touched her heart. She grabbed a book on penguins from the reading area and handed it to Jimmy. She turned to see Dillon at the doorway studying the room's decorations.

"I called Gilby this morning to find out how he was feeling," he whispered to her.

She beamed with happiness when she saw him but now after hearing that he was only concerned about Grandpa, her satisfaction plummeted. "Well, he's doing great, he even helped me paint the house."

"Yeah, that's what he said. His voice even sounds better. Listen, I don't want to take your time. I'm here to help deliver some stuff to the school." He turned toward the hall.

Seeing him again stirred her emotions and she didn't want to see him go. She wanted to tell him how great the house looks with fresh paint and just how good Grandpa really was doing. And about Pup. He needed to know what was happening in the tower room. She, at least, needed his opinion about what she should do next. He always knew what to do.

"Are you going to be around for a while?" she asked looking at the clock, then Dillon. "I have a break at ten. There are some things I'd like to tell you."

He looked at his watch. "I'm not sure, but I think so. Bye."

Knowing ten minutes went by fast, Taylor raced down to the office to find Dillon at recess time. The secretary said he left the building. He did, however, leave a message in her mailbox.

She read the note in a whisper, "My work here didn't take long. Part of the day I'm spending on paperwork. If you still want to talk, stop by my place after work. D.N."

Not his place again, she thought. She didn't want to even think about what a fool she made of herself going there the first time.

However, she grew tired of being frightened in her own home. She had to talk it over with him, get his feedback.

"What a beautiful man," said Johnna behind her. "Too bad he's gay."

Taylor chuckled. "He's not gay."

"No, probably not. He's probably just married, or nearly. Guys like that usually aren't available. Only in romance novels. Did you happen to see him today?"

"Yes, he stopped by my classroom in time to see Jimmy stand on his desk. Well, that's not entirely true, I stopped him before he could reach the top."

Johnna shook her head. "That Jimmy. What a character."

Taylor was glad the subject changed as she didn't want to tell her that she planned to see him after school. She left Johnna with her thoughts on Jimmy.

———

Dillon opened the door to her that afternoon with a breathy sigh.

"You, okay?"

"Several hours in front of the computer screen has done me in. Come in and take a seat."

Taylor took a seat at the table. Dillon closed his laptop and stretched out on the bed with folded hands behind his head. The silence was deafening. Taylor didn't know quite how to begin, knowing she didn't want to blurt out her problems the very first thing. The last thing she wanted was for him to think her needy, especially when he made it clear that he was done helping them.

"It was nice to see you in your element today. The kids are cute, but I think I'd be going upriver for murder after about one hour with the desk climber."

She smiled. Oh, she'd missed him, and a lump formed in her

throat. She rubbed her face as if to clear her emotions. Momentarily it worked, until she focused on the long legs stretched out across the bed.

She cleared her throat. "You should see the house; it's beautiful in yellow with white trim. We did it. Grandpa and I did it. I'm very proud. Of course, we aren't quite finished but will be in time."

"Did you spill any paint on your skirt?"

"Actually, not a drop."

They were quiet again. She glanced out the window, then at Dillon. She caught his eyes scanning her figure. She sat up straighter and started to wring her hands.

"Let's get out of here," Dillon said. "I'm hungry. Let's get dinner. We can get something to take home to Gilby, too."

After a quick call to Grandpa, to tell him she'd be late, they moved to the door. The phone rang and Dillon sat on the bed to answer it. "Oh, Mommy Dearest," he said, smiling. "How are you, Casey?"

Dillon hadn't said much about his mother. Taylor sat back down, interested. Their talk consisted mainly of business, what Dillon had been doing. He asked about someone named Steven. She knew he didn't have any brothers, so she assumed it was probably Casey's significant other.

He turned and looked at Taylor and said abruptly, "Casey, I've got to go. I have company. No, it isn't Jeff. Later. Bye."

"Guess you didn't want to tell her you had a woman in your room, huh?"

"Guess not."

Because he had said the words without a smile, it made her feel sad he didn't want to tell his mother about her. She wished to heaven she didn't care about what Dillon thought, but something inside told her she did care. A lot.

At the restaurant, their conversation went so well that he even talked of taking her to the falls one day. He also wanted to show her how the resort was coming along. Before she knew it, dessert was served, and Taylor realized she hadn't broached the subject of her house. She still didn't quite know how to start the conversation.

"So, what else did Grandpa tell you when you called this morning?" she asked.

"That you haven't named Pup yet."

She smiled thinking of some of Grandpa's suggestions, then said, "Did Grandpa tell you he's been barking a lot? That he's a good watch dog?"

Dillon leaned in closer. "He's been barking? At what?"

"Well, that's one thing I wanted to talk to you about. Weird stuff has been happening again."

He leaned back and sighed. However, he looked like he was disappointed in her. Perhaps he didn't understand what she was saying.

"Pup has been barking at the tower room. Many times, I've found the light on and the door open, and neither one of us has been near the room. It's kind of like the place is haunted or something."

Dillon leaned forward again, "Now, Gilby didn't say anything about this. Why wouldn't he tell me?'

"I don't think Grandpa knows much of what's going on. Because he sleeps so soundly, he doesn't always hear Pup barking at night. Then-"

"I don't believe you, Taylor."

She couldn't have heard him right. "What did you say?"

"I said I don't believe you."

Feeling like she'd been slapped in the face, she sat up a little taller and said, "Now, why would I lie to you?"

"Because you want to use me again."

Her ears must be deceiving her. He couldn't possibly mean what he said. "I can't believe you're saying this, Dillon."

"It's because I've been there and done that more than once in my lifetime. You grow a little jaded after a while when people just want you for your money."

"Your money? I want your *money?*"

"For my brawn, for a commitment that leads to money."

These words brought her crashing back to reality. A reality that didn't include a trip to the falls, or a visit to the resort, or even friendship for that matter.

"Why you egotistical… You egotistical…" With a labored sigh she added, "I wish you were a carpenter like I first thought."

He snickered. "I can't believe you mean that."

She stood up, opened her purse, and threw a twenty-dollar bill on the table. "How dare you insinuate that I'm lying? Money has never been a turn on to me." She looked around, then sat down and lowered her voice.

"Now I must tell you that today I didn't expect to use you." Her bottom lip quivered, and she fought back the tears. "All I wanted was for you to give me some advice about what could possibly be happening in the house. That's all, *advice.*" She felt zapped of energy. "Please take me to my car."

When they arrived at her car, he reached across her and opened her door. "You know you could sell the house."

"Thanks, but no thanks," she said with a low voice and shut the pickup door.

CHAPTER 14

*T*aylor bought two baseball bats, one for the main floor and another for her bedroom. A bat would have to do because she didn't trust herself, or someone else, with a gun. She decided that if the tables turned on her during a struggle, she'd rather be hit with a bat than shot with a gun. Also, she became so cross since her meeting with Dillon that the intruder best beware. Her anger made her a contender to dread.

She moved the bat from behind her bedroom door to between her mattresses and then back again, while wondering why whoever was terrifying her enough to move didn't just ask her to leave. She might think about an offer rather than go through this.

Then she remembered there was one person that suggested she move. A man named Dillon Nash. Nevertheless, the thought was insane because he could offer her a lot of money for the house if he really wanted it. She shook her head to stop herself from thinking about him.

She laid the baseball bat under the bed, then headed downstairs to where Grandpa sat reading the newspaper.

He looked at her over his glasses. "Did I tell you Dillon called?"

"No, you didn't. How's he doing? Making more money?"

"Well, you sound a little testy. He's helped us a lot. You should be grateful to him."

Her mind went back to their last meeting. Dillon thought the house was too much for her and she should sell it. Well, she would show him, and she was by everything she did to repair the house. After all, real estate was a fine investment, and the house would be worth much more after restored to its former glory.

Calvin had a week and a half left before he moved out. She couldn't wait to get a better look at his quarters. She may possibly redo it one day and rent it out. If that wasn't good business sense, then she didn't know what was.

"Didn't you hear me, Taylor?" Grandpa looked at her like she'd lost her marbles.

"I'm thankful for what he has done for us, Grandpa," she replied hoping this would close the subject. Just in case it didn't, she started to leave the room.

"He asked how you were doing."

She stopped in her tracks and looked down at her feet. "Yes, but he didn't call me to find out. He called you when he knew I was at work."

He picked up his newspaper. "Oh, I see what the problem is."

Mocking her grandfather silently, she walked into the kitchen to fix something to eat. Before she turned on the light she saw, through the window, that someone was lurking in the shadows.

Her anger and frustration popped like a bubble. With a fearful pounding heart, she checked to make sure the door was locked and closed the curtains. After turning out the kitchen light, she carefully peeked out the corners of the blinds but didn't see anything. Sitting on a chair in the dark kitchen, she listened for sounds of intrusion, while Pup lay dozing at her feet. Thankfully, nothing happened.

Leftovers made a quick meal and Grandpa made his way back to the couch and TV. Taylor jumped when the landline telephone rang. It was a hang-up call, and it took more than a few moments for her heart to resume a normal beat. She wondered how long her heart would last beating as hard as it had in the last hour.

She took Johnna's advice and called the police department to ask if they had teenagers or gangs in Trillium to worry about. She was unrealistically disappointed when they told her that the only problem in Trillium Falls was bicycle theft.

As Taylor sat down the phone, she heard knocking at the back door. With breath bursting in and out, she wondered if she should ignore it, or see who it was.

After a moment, she grabbed a baseball bat and asked who was there. It was Jerry and she couldn't remember being so happy to see anyone. Resting the bat against a corner, she opened the door and happily drew him in by the arm.

"How's everybody doing?"

"Oh, fine. Fine. I'm afraid you're a moment too late, we've just finished dinner."

"I certainly didn't come to impose on you."

"Of course not." She looked around the kitchen. "Can I get you some cookies, coffee, a soda or something?"

"No, not right now, but thanks. I was in the mood for a game, hoping Gilby would be up to it."

"Do you play pinochle? I love pinochle," she said, over zealously.

"I never thought that you'd ever want to join us. Sure. Is Gilby up to it?"

She nodded. Playing cards was not something she thought of either. She was only glad to have someone else in the house. The more the merrier. She scurried to find the cards.

"The cards are in that catch-all drawer there," said Grandpa walking in. He made his way into the kitchen.

"What's the baseball bat doing on the floor?" Jerry looked at Grandpa and Grandpa looked to Taylor.

"Oh, the bat. Yes. I'm doing a segment on softball at school."

"Don't they have PE teachers to do that these days?" Jerry asked.

"Lots of budget cuts coming up," she answered with a nervous laugh and handed the cards to Grandpa.

"You didn't tell me about the PE department being cut," Grandpa looked from the cards to Taylor.

She sighed. "We'll talk about that later, Grandpa. We don't want to bore Jerry."

"No, that's okay, go ahead, don't let me interrupt."

"Please, later." Her voice had a note of seriousness in it that caused both men to eye her again.

"PMS," Grandpa mumbled to Jerry. Jerry nodded while looking at the stack of cards.

"Every time a woman raises her voice doesn't mean she has PMS, Grandpa."

"I've lived longer than you, I know these things. Who wants to deal?"

"I will," Jerry returned, then wisely changed the subject. "What's new around here?"

"Calvin should be leaving us soon. Wait, you probably already knew that," said Grandpa.

Jerry finished dealing then looked up at Grandpa. "Why no. I'm surprised he's not staying, because he has such a good arrangement here. Where's he going?"

"He had the perfect arrangement all right," said Grandpa. "I did more work in the yard than he did. We told him to leave."

"Well, you're exaggerating a little, Grandpa, but true, he didn't do much. It's just that at this point in our lives we don't need a boarder, especially someone who's making our financial burden a bit heavier. Maybe someday we can redo the place and then rent it out and make a few more bucks. But we're not ready yet. I'm sorry for Calvin, but he's not our responsibility."

"That's a good idea, Granddaughter. Real estate is always a good investment, and it will make this place worth more to make part of it a rental."

Her heart felt light with her grandfather's approval. "I take the bid at 250."

"Pass," shot in Grandpa.

"260," voiced Jerry. "You guys seem to have a lot of confidence in this house. You think you'll be able to rent it?"

"Sure, it would be cheap rent for somebody. Taylor, first bidder calls trump."

"Trump is spades."

"I mean it may be hard to rent again with the history of this house," added Jerry.

Grandpa rubbed his chin, then answered, "Well that's what it is, just history. People will forget, especially when they watch the house come to life. It's already looking much better with a coat of paint."

"No more problems then, huh?"

"Uh," Grandpa said, "It's going to continue to be hard for Taylor to do much on the house without me. But I'm feeling better all the time and she'll get my help."

Taylor looked up from her cards and Grandpa winked at her. She returned his wink with a full smile. He now voiced what she used to only say in faith. It felt good. Yet, when she looked across the table, she saw skepticism in Jerry's eyes. His next words confirmed it.

"The gossip is that you'll have trouble in this house, too."

She wondered where he got off trying to scare them, especially Grandpa. She tried hard not to let him know he'd upset her. "The trouble we've had, Jerry, we've brought with us. Grandpa lost his wife and was ill before we ever heard of this place."

"I'm only relating gossip."

When neither Taylor nor Grandpa responded, he began again but this time with a chuckle. "No ghosts or goblins, huh?"

Grandpa looked up from his cards. "Pup barks at the wind, that's about all. What did you say trump was again, Taylor?"

"Spades."

Jerry directed his gaze at Taylor. "You've got to think this stuff about the house was all a hoax since nothing happens anymore. Right?"

She took a moment to answer. She had been willing to tell Dillon about this mess, why shouldn't she tell Jerry? He, like Dillon, could have ideas or answers as to what they could do, too. Yet, in two seconds her instincts, or intuition, told her he was a man of questions, not answers. Besides, what kind of logic did he have trying to upset the two of them? This was not the first time he emptied his mouth to Grandpa. Her grandfather was very ill at the time, and she still didn't forgive him for that. She would not enter another discussion about this house with Jerry and especially not with Grandpa present.

"Right," she answered firmly.

Jerry looked at her with squinting eyes, which probably meant he didn't believe her.

Dillon's distrust of Jerry came to mind. She believed that Jerry was a simpler man than Dillon had thought. She considered him a man with a big mouth that also had a benevolent side to him. He showed no real interest in her, only coming over to see her convalescing grandfather.

To Grandpa, he shared stories, jokes, and smiles. He even gave King more attention than he gave her, remembering he even fed him, albeit without permission.

Jerry stayed until bedtime. The pinochle game was fun and distracting, so much so that she almost forgot about the tower room until she passed it on her way to bed. Thankfully, nothing was amiss, and her sleep went undisturbed.

CHAPTER 15

The following day, Taylor agonized over leaving Grandpa home alone. At least when she was away at school it was during the daylight. She felt worse than usual because she'd stayed after school for a meeting until almost dark. Her stomach ached and she knew if things stayed the same, she'd have a full-blown ulcer in a year's time.

Nevertheless, there was nothing she could do about her circumstances. She wanted to keep her job in Trillium Falls and the house. The last thing she wanted to do was move. Rehashing it in her mind didn't do any good.

When Taylor pulled into the driveway the tower room light shined out into the darkness, and her heart picked up a beat. She thought about going to the shed, or looking in her trunk for a blunt instrument, but thought it would be more expedient to check on Grandpa. He could already be hurt.

She jumped onto the porch and met Pup there. Panic consumed her, because after King disappeared, they agreed that Pup shouldn't be out by himself.

Taylor bit her lip to focus on opening the door. Then tears, anger, and a multitude of emotions ripped through her as she fumbled with the lock and opened the door.

Grandpa and Dillon sat on the couch watching something on television. She backed against the door and started to cry with relief and something akin to pain. "I…I didn't see your truck."

"Not out there."

By then she had both men's full attention and Pup's, too. "What's wrong, Granddaughter?"

"Oh…Oh, it was a hard meeting." She was tired of twisting the truth.

"Don't take it so hard. Believe me, I've had my share of irate parents and frustrating individual educational plan meetings." Grandpa struggled to get up to go to her. Dillon put a hand on Grandpa's thigh to stop him. Instead, Dillon went over and gently hand guided her into the kitchen.

Dillon turned to face her. "I know how you stand up to me when you want to, so I don't believe for two seconds some parent could upset you like this."

Taylor rubbed the tears off her chin with the sleeve of her shirt. She looked up at his sullen face, then watched him cross his arms. Her tears dried instantly, and her chin went up. "I was imagining the tower room light was on and the great big dragon came down to get my grandfather and alas! My dog was outside waiting to get taken, or poisoned, and I was afraid. But Lady Taylor only imagined it all so that the handsome Prince Dillon would come and live with her, and she would get *all* his fortune." Her voice sobered, "What are you doing here, Dillon?"

He rubbed a hand through his hair then glanced at the ceiling. "I started thinking about what you said, and I did a drive by and noticed that the tower room light was on and you weren't home. I called a taxi and had it drop me down the street. I walked here."

She snorted.

"I'm sorry, okay? I'm sorry." With a quieter voice, he said, "You must see that you need to tell Gilby what's going on, so he's able to protect himself when he's here alone."

Her eyes welled up with tears again. "I don't want him to regress."

"I know it's hard for you, still you've got to keep him informed."

Grabbing her hands, he led her to the kitchen chairs and sat down. "Listen, we're going to tell Gilby what's going on. Everything. Then I'm going to be spending some time in the tower room. I want to get to the bottom of this."

"Why would you do that Dillon?"

"All I'll say right now is that I have my reasons."

"What's that supposed to mean?"

He stubbornly stood there working the muscle in his jaw. "You'll have to trust me."

She sighed and said, "You were here before, and nothing happened."

"I know, that's why I left the truck at the motel. I'll keep out of sight."

She rubbed the back of her neck. "It might work, but I don't know about telling Grandpa everything."

"He's healthier now. He can deal with it. He'll be okay. We need teamwork to get to the bottom of this."

Taylor nodded.

"Get me a sleeping bag and bring it to the tower room, *after* you've talked to Gilby."

"Dillon, thanks," she said not looking at him.

He didn't reply.

After some searching, she found the sleeping bags and shook them briskly. She also put some chocolate chip cookies in a sandwich bag for Dillon.

Dillon sat on the floor of the tower room, his eyes closed and back against the wall. Taylor dropped two sleeping bags at his feet, and he looked up abruptly. "I only need one bag."

"The other one is for me."

For a moment, he opened his eyes wide then closed them again. "You don't need to be in the middle of things."

"I can't pay you what you're worth, Dillon. I can go through this with you, or at least learn what to do from you. You can't be babysitting us all the time."

She looked around the room and felt chilled. "Maybe we could play cards or something."

Dillon put his elbows on his knees and rubbed his face. "Solitaire. What did Gilby say about all this?"

"He didn't say much, but his face showed concern. He said he was glad you were here. I imagine he'll think about it and get mad because I didn't say something sooner."

"Rightly so."

"You know it's hard to know what to do. I felt I should protect Grandpa from this. Stress isn't good for him."

The landline rang and Taylor ran to get it. The silent caller hung up. On her way back to tell Dillon about the calls, she noticed she was not nearly as upset as the last time it happened and he wasn't here.

"Good. They probably don't think I'm here. Don't tell *anyone* I'm here, even if someone calls for me. Got it?"

"Of course. I'll tell Grandpa."

"Gilby told me you asked Calvin to move out. Has he?"

"No, and I don't see any signs of it yet."

"What do you mean?"

"Well, we haven't seen any boxes going in or out, for one."

"I wonder if he thinks you'll feel sorry for him and let him stay."

"I doubt that. He doesn't even look my way when we pass each other."

"And how about Garcia?"

"He comes around. We played pinochle last night."

"Why do you let him in?" he asked disgusted.

"He comes to see Grandpa, not me."

"Any weird behavior?"

"He asks too many questions, but I think that's just his nature. He also says too many things to Grandpa about what people are saying about the house. I don't think he should. It might scare him."

Dillon's eyebrows furrowed. "How's his behavior with you?"

"He's here to see Grandpa, no doubt about it," she said firmly.

Dillon shook his head then rubbed his face again. "Just don't tell him I'm here."

"Fair enough."

"Was he here when the hang up call was made?"

She thought a moment. "No, I don't think so."

He sat down on one of the sleeping bags, sat up straighter and looked her full in the eye. "You seem disappointed that Jerry is only interested in Gilby."

She laughed out loud.

He stood up and began to run his hand along the panels of the wall. "I wasn't trying to be funny."

She didn't think he was being funny, only ignorant. She stretched out her hand, palm up. "How do you think I could possibly get a man from Trillium Falls interested in me, when I live in this *haunted* house?"

He turned to look at her, crossed his arms and leaned back against the wall. "Jerry enters this house."

"Yes, but then so do you and that doesn't mean you want me for a girlfriend, now does it?" Somehow, the saying of it made her feel inferior. This time she rubbed her face then lifted her chin and began again. "I suppose with time people will forget the rumors as they watch the house turn into something that doesn't look so scary. That's why I don't want to get the police involved in this mess. I don't want the town to continue to believe something's going on here."

"Somebody may know that. That you're not calling the police for a reason."

"Yeah, like I don't call the police because I want to have a boyfriend. You're not trying to pick a fight, are you?"

"No," he answered with exasperation. "I think maybe somebody thinks you aren't calling the police for a reason. They're probably thinking they can scare you out of here without any outside police intervention. They're probably thrilled about that."

Taylor, chilled, straightened up and crossed her arms. "You said they. Do you think there's more than one?"

"I don't know anything for sure, I'm just speculating."

"As long as you're speculating, what do you think *they* think is my reason for not calling the police?"

Dillon smiled, then said, "You're a woman and a man wouldn't have a clue as to why you do things."

She believed Dillon just wanted to cheer her up, and she smiled, wishing she had something to throw. Dillon kneeled before her and kissed the top of her head. Looking up at him, she smiled again.

"You are not sleeping in here because you won't sleep, and you've got school tomorrow. Leave the door open so I'll have more heat in here. I won't be leaving the house for a while, so I want you to go by my motel room and pick up some things for me tomorrow before school. Put the stuff in one of your book bags so if anybody's watching they won't see anything unusual."

"Sure, sure." Turning to go, she said softly, "Thanks, Dillon, it means a lot to...to us."

———

TAYLOR LEFT THE HOUSE FORTY-FIVE MINUTES EARLIER THAN USUAL. Even though she didn't see any witnesses, she felt guilty of a crime by going into Dillon's room without him.

She looked about the room and at the list of items he requested. After she packed the bag, she grabbed a Levi shirt, hugged it to herself and danced around the room. It struck her then that she loved him, because people just didn't go around dancing with other people's clothes without a reason. She had so much more to learn about this enigma of a man, and she hoped she wasn't doomed to a world of heartache.

Back at the house with a few minutes to spare, she took Dillon's things to him.

"You didn't ask for any weapons. Should I get a knife or something? What do you think?"

He shook his head. "Sorry, Taylor, but boyfriend or no boyfriend, I will call the police if I have to," he said pointing to his cell phone.

"Yeah, I realize that," she said and left the room, coming back with a baseball bat. "Try using this first. You wouldn't want me to go without a boyfriend, now, would you?" She left the room with a wink and a shake of her hair.

It lifted her spirits to have another able body in the house. She totally enjoyed the moment, the moment she was living in, valuing it highly, because she knew it wouldn't last.

CHAPTER 16

a dog barked and Taylor woke in an instant, but it took a moment for her to focus and realize what she heard was Pup. Springing up to a sitting position, she listened for other sounds to help her understand what happened. *The tower room.*

Pup continued to bark, and she wondered why Dillon allowed it. The dog could be silenced easily enough. She started to worry about Dillon and went to investigate.

Taylor remembered she gave her baseball bat to Dillon, so defenseless, she stepped gingerly down the hall. After nearly bumping into Grandpa at the entrance of the tower room, she held up her hand for him to wait while she went ahead to look for Dillon.

The light from the hall cast a dim light on Dillon and Pup. He stood against the wall watching the dog move about the room sniffing, growling, and emitting an occasional bark. He put a finger up to his mouth to silence her.

At their presence, Pup's behavior altered immediately. She could feel his tail hitting her legs in greeting. After a moment, she stepped back into the hall and told Grandpa to go back to bed. A barking dog shouldn't keep them all up, she'd whispered to him, and he agreed and shuffled off to bed.

Going back to Dillon, she pushed her hair off her face and raised her eyebrows in question. "Well?"

"Pup's going to be a great watch dog. Actually, already is," he whispered close to her ear.

She nodded.

"First I heard some footsteps. I'm not sure where they came from. It almost sounded like they came from the hall. But that couldn't be. Pup heard it, too, and started barking."

He sat down on the sleeping bag. "Go back to bed, I doubt if we'll hear anything else tonight."

She came to that conclusion too and turned to leave.

"Taylor?" he spoke softly.

"Yeah?" she answered in the same manner.

"Next time wear a robe. With the way the light shines in from the hallway I can see right through your gown."

"Oh. Sorry."

"Don't be."

———

DILLON DIDN'T ALWAYS STAY IN THE TOWER ROOM, SHE NOTED, WHEN he came out to shower and have breakfast. He joined Grandpa for toaster waffles and a slice of ham.

The two of them talked about the recent basketball game like it was just another day. Her grandfather didn't seem concerned at all about the news she gave him the night before. All this time, she kept it to herself with tension and ulcers brewing in her middle, afraid he would only feel the same.

With a sigh, she realized that if she had told Grandpa in the first place, they could have worked together finding an answer to this mess without anyone else getting involved. She now felt foolish looking at her grandfather as he heartily ate his breakfast.

"What's the sigh for, Taylor?" Dillon looked over to where she filled her book bag with a tablet, folders and a manual needed for school.

Right, like she'd tell him the real reason. Instead, she said, "I was wondering if you wanted me to get you anything on my way home."

"Relax, not today."

Grandpa cleared his throat. "Dillon, I'd like to thank you for coming to our aid. I'm afraid I'm not much help to myself or Taylor these days and it bothers me that I'm not the man I used to be. Now that I know about all this weird stuff going on, I don't really know what we'd do without you. It does my heart good, in this day and age, to see a man come to someone's aid like you're doing. My burden's lifted considerably, I can't thank you enough. I don't really feel like I have anything to fear now."

Dillon wiggled uncomfortably in his chair; his face solemn when Grandpa spoke. The two men sat in silence finishing their meal.

By the time Taylor grabbed her car keys and said goodbye, she realized that Grandpa felt the way she did yesterday, relieved at having another able body in the house to help. Now she understood why Grandpa didn't appear affected by the news she sprung at him about the tower room. When she considered the way Dillon squirmed when Grandpa gave his thanks, she figured he probably felt a bit trapped. She decided she would really try to be helpful in any way she could.

She began by making a homemade meal. After stopping to purchase the needed items at the neighborhood market, she spent the next hour chopping up chicken breasts and making chicken burritos. Next, she put together a layered green salad with left over bacon and sliced eggs she'd boiled while she sautéed the chicken.

For dessert, she remembered a cheesecake mix in the cupboard, which only took a short time to put together.

After flipping through the mail and getting Grandpa situated with dinner, she took a plate up to Dillon. He sat on the sleeping bag where she'd seen him last night, only this time he played solitaire on his laptop computer.

"I thought I smelled something good cooking." He reached up to take the plate offered. "This is certainly worth sitting up here all day."

"Anything happen out of the ordinary?" Taylor asked and sat down beside him.

He shook his head in answer. He devoured the food quickly and Taylor realized that she hadn't made any arrangements with him for lunch. She'd remember the next time.

"These burritos are better than mine. Good job. Thanks."

"Well, I remembered that you liked them. Seems like everybody's are just a little bit different. I have dessert, too."

"Great. How was your day? Entertain me."

"Well, I'm a little concerned about a girl in my class. She's been making things up, like at recess she pointed to a third-grade boy and said he was her brother. Yet, I happen to know she only has sisters, and they are both younger than she is. Then one time she told me her grandmother died, but come to find out she didn't."

"So young, too. Tough," he added setting his plate down, then popped open the can of soda with one hand.

"The counselor said it's not uncommon. Sometimes a child's life is so burdened or boring that they create another one."

"A few hours ago, I was so bored, I almost had a brother," he said and smiled.

"I bet you were. Listen, I'm sorry you're wasting the day on us, and I appreciate it."

He nodded but looked away from her.

After a few moments of silence, she asked, "More to eat? Dessert?"

"Later on."

"Okay, I'll get it later. Dillon?"

He looked back at her. "Hmm?"

"I don't want you to think that I want you here to trap you into being with me. I must admit it offends me when you think that's what I want to do."

Bending his knees to his chest, he propped his arms on them. "I need to tell you something, Taylor. I suppose I'm getting paranoid as I'm getting older. Or, more cautious. My experience is that the women I've had in my life seem to want me for what I can give them, more than for who I am as a man. Something or other happens and I learn it's the clubs, or the shopping sprees, the jewelry or financial independence that I can give them.

"My last girlfriend, her name's Liz, actually had the gall to say she wanted a nurse and a nanny to take care of our children so she wouldn't have to. She was furious that she'd slipped and said it in my presence when we had some friends over. Perhaps it would have been different if she wanted a career, but she couldn't think of a thing she wanted to do but be my wife. I broke up with her shortly after. To save face, she..." He rubbed his face. "Never mind."

Looking at him closely now, she found his message funny, and chuckled.

Dillon slapped one of his knees. "Now, why do you think that's funny?"

"Sh! Sh! Keep your voice down or Casper won't come out tonight."

He looked around the room and nodded.

"Sounds like your money has been a curse to you," she said, and another chuckle slipped out.

"Curse is not a funny word, Taylor."

"It's just if I was going to use you, it wouldn't be for money."

"I know, it would be for protection from Casper," he said evenly through clenched teeth.

"Hey, wait a minute, I don't use people. You came here on your own accord. I never insinuated that you should move in here. That's more than a person should ask." She crossed her arms and looked down at her feet.

Dillon crossed his arms, too.

"That's the truth." She crossed her heart.

"So, what was so funny?"

"Oh, Dillon," she said with a sigh. "You're not exactly an ugly guy. I've never thought about using you for your money, but I have thought about you, uh…physically."

"Oh, I know that men use women for money, too." Then his eyebrows furrowed. "What did you say?"

She fanned her fingers out in front of her face. "Dillon, what I'm saying is I can't imagine cold women being linked to you. Oh, never mind."

"Beautiful, but cold. Which doesn't describe you."

"Don't make fun of my looks."

"God, Taylor."

"I think I have it worse than you do. Now don't take me wrong, my grandfather took me in when I really needed him and I'm happy to do the same, but who'd want to pick me up here at this place? Then if he did step inside, survived, and wanted to marry me, he probably wouldn't want my grandfather to be part of the package."

"Yeah, not a pretty picture. You know if you shopped out of town maybe you could get a guy in Boise," he said with a grin.

She playfully slugged his shoulder. "Well, for that matter Dillon, there is somebody out there for you, too. You're smart as a whip, you're good with your hands, and you have a sensitive side to you, judging by the way you care about Grandpa." He's a good man, she told herself. A good man and sadly, she loved him. But she didn't want to let herself go there.

"*And* you have money," she added.

"Ha!" He pulled her over onto his lap. She felt as comfortable as if she was made to fit there. He kissed her brow then looked across at the wall apparently lost in thought. His features grew harder to see as night approached and the room had darkened.

After a few minutes, she wondered how he could hold her without wanting more. *Her* heart picked up a beat, then her mind went back to when they first spent time together. He seemed hot to touch her then. As time progressed, she wondered about his new reserve. Perhaps he'd gotten to know her better and didn't feel an attraction to her, or he's refrained due to his respect for her grandfather.

"What are you thinking about?" she asked softly.

"I'm thinking about my brother," he said with a smile.

"Are you that bored, Dillon? Maybe I can help with that."

At this moment, she really didn't care what he felt about her, she wanted to be closer to him than skin. She lifted her head and he watched while her lips touched his. He had perfect lips, full enough to be sensuous yet enough firmness in them to be supreme at the skill of softly sucking hers. She was the first to use her tongue and he moaned and overran hers to get his across her lips. They stayed like that for some time, Dillon becoming as eager to kiss, as he was earlier to eat.

Yet, it wasn't enough for Taylor, she wanted more but Dillon slowed down. "You make me crazy, Dillon. Crazy," she whispered.

Her words moved Dillon to lift her out of his lap and onto the sleeping bag. He covered her with his body putting one elbow on each side of her shoulders. "You know, Gilby came up here twice today. He could come again."

"Gilby who?" she replied and snuggled under him.

"The man who's keeping you from getting married, because he'll have to live with you and your husband."

It took a moment for the meaning of his words to hit her. "Oh, him," she said with a perturbed sigh.

"Can't very well use me for sex if Gilby might come in."

"Oh, Dillon." She felt such emotion that she knew it must shine out of her eyes. And she felt heat, burning heat. However, she felt the temperature go down when she finally considered what he'd said.

Taylor wasn't a total idiot. She knew she couldn't have a physical relationship with Dillon and just walk away. At least not with her heart intact. She needed to think this through.

When she pulled herself upright her legs shook and she didn't know if she could stand, let alone walk. Steadying herself against the wall she said, "I might be back at midnight. Until then I'll get that dessert, okay?"

Dillon looked at her intently and she would have given the world to know what he was thinking. He said nothing to reveal himself, only a soft, "Okay."

The cheesecake looked good to Taylor. That's when she remembered she hadn't eaten dinner. She'd been too worried about Dillon and Grandpa eating to think about her own welfare. She took some time to think, eat, then tidy up the kitchen before she went back up to the tower room with dessert.

She really did need to catch up on some schoolwork before morning, she told Dillon, and then it was time to head for bed. She turned Pup into the tower room and said goodnight. "Hope you can sleep," Dillon said.

Toss and turn is what she did. Just shy of midnight she made her way to the tower room. Dillon didn't seem surprised to see her.

Taylor handed Pup a rawhide bone, then stood before Dillon. He took the other rolled up sleeping bag and spread it out, then laid on it and motioned for her to join him. Once she did, he covered them both with the other sleeping bag.

"Couldn't sleep, huh?"

"Nope."

It felt wonderful to hold him. Most hugs she'd had were given lightly, not amounting to anything more than a pat on the back. She could tell Dillon's hugs were not intended to lead to anything sexual. They were all encompassing, making her feel cared for and protected as well. She knew of no one else in the world that could embrace her quite this way and she became misty-eyed thinking about it.

Little light came in from the hall making it hard to see the face she traced with her finger. "You are beautiful, Dillon," she said scratching the sandpaper-like stubble on his chin which added to his appeal.

Pup dropped his bone and went to their heads. He sniffed and tried to lick their faces. Taylor laughed and Dillon swatted at him.

"Lay down, Pup, lay down," he ordered as sternly as he could in a whisper. Pup flopped back down and renewed his ardor for the bone.

"You've got to name that dog, Taylor."

"Um hum," she said, and Dillon positioned himself over her again.

"Now where was I? Oh yeah. And I think you're...you're... wonderful. Green eyes full of fire," he returned her compliment with a wide smile revealing even white teeth that she touched. He kissed her nose.

She would have liked to have heard beautiful, or pretty, instead, but at the point where Dillon began tracing the v of her collarbone with his tongue she didn't really care.

"You taste good," he said and then went back up to capture her lips less gentle than before. He took her mouth and gave his tongue urgently.

"You sure now, Taylor? You sure this is okay?"

"Well, what I'm sure about is that I don't want this moment to end. Ever," she said solemnly, just above a whisper. "Ever," she said again.

"I don't want to hurt you. I'll try not to hurt you," he said in a whisper.

She hoped with all her heart he meant emotionally as well as physically.

"Relax now, relax," he coaxed her. He coaxed well but let go when a flash of bright light filled the room.

Her first thought was that it was Grandpa and even though now a woman and not a child, she dreaded getting caught. When Pup growled and Dillon put his hand over her mouth to silence her, she knew it wasn't Grandpa. She had been so caught up in the moment, ever since dinner, that she hadn't even thought about the tower room being anything but a haven. Now her thoughts cleared, and her heart began to pound, but for an altogether different reason.

After her eyes adjusted to the bright room, Taylor sat up and pulled the sleeping bag up to her chin. Dillon already shot up and looked down the hall. Pup followed him with a single bark, then did nothing but sit at the doorway looking up at Dillon. He looked down at the dog, then back at her.

"I didn't hear anyone coming down the hall. Did you?"

"No."

"Pup doesn't seem to think there's anyone to chase. I'll go check on Gilby."

He left her there alone and she looked from wall to wall to doorway in fear. To her consolation, he was back immediately.

"Gilby's sound asleep," he said, first pacing, then after he pushed back his hair with a hand, he looked about the room. He turned abruptly and went to the light switch.

"The switch is in the off position." When he flipped it up the light went off and when he pushed it back down it didn't come back on. "Did you notice that the light switch was backward?" he asked her.

"No." This was too scary. She clutched at the bag.

"Go get me a new light bulb."

"All by myself?" she asked, not too sure of the situation.

"I'm going to check the fuse box. Take Pup with you. We've got to figure this out."

She scurried to get the job done quickly, Pup at her heels, happily in pursuit. At every creak of the house, she turned sharply and nearly screamed when the refrigerator started up.

Back with a hundred-watt bulb, she handed it to Dillon, which he traded for a flashlight. He grabbed a stool from Gilby's room to stand on. "Point the light up while I change the bulb."

"Sure."

He stepped down and attempted to turn the light back on. When it didn't come back on, he asked if she was sure the bulb was good.

"I have every reason to think it's good. I have another pack of sixties you can try."

She was off again but to no avail because the light still wouldn't come on.

"Looks like our culprit has some electrical knowledge." He turned to look at her. "I'd like to check out Calvin's wing."

"You don't think Calvin has anything to do with this, do you?" she asked skeptically.

"No, he's a drunk. Too much is happening when he's probably passed out or unable to even stand. I haven't ruled out the possibility of someone getting past him though."

"Set up another card game with Garcia. I want to hear the questions he asks and what he says. I'll hide somewhere so he can't see me."

Taylor crossed her arms and shook her head. "Jerry's a nice man, a friend to Grandpa."

He too grew impatient. "This is serious business, Taylor. We need to check out everything. Now be sure and remember not to tell *anyone* I'm here."

"Of course."

"Good. Now go to bed but leave Pup, his ears are better than mine."

With all that had transpired in the last twenty minutes, she knew there wouldn't be any snuggling in the tower room now. The danger, and the conflict about Jerry between them, popped the romantic mood like a bubble.

CHAPTER 17

The following day, Taylor climbed over the fence to Jerry's backyard. She headed around to the front door, checking her tennis shoes for mud as she went. She didn't see a car parked in the driveway and she bit her lip with uncertainty when she knocked at the door. Then she rang the doorbell.

She stepped over the flowerbed and cupped her hands around her eyes, peering in the front window to find some evidence of life.

She thought Jerry made a fair wage but from where she stood now, she wasn't so sure. The house, sparsely decorated, had one old stuffed chair in the living room, a TV on the floor and a dining table with one chair next to it.

Glad she came prepared, she climbed back onto the porch and reached into her pocket for a piece of paper and pen to write a note. When Jerry pulled up, she pushed the paper back into her pocket.

He drove a late model four-wheel-drive pickup. She shook her head as he climbed out, thinking he sure didn't know how to spend his money. He turned and smiled at her, then reached across the seat and grabbed a leather duffel bag.

"Taylor," he said with a nod.

"Hi, Jerry. I was hoping to catch you home."

"Yeah, good timing."

"You been away?" she asked pointing at his duffel bag.

"No. Uh…I was at the gym."

Good thing she wasn't his mother, she thought, surveying his slim body. She'd be telling him to use that money on something for his house. "Oh."

"What can I do for you?"

She waited for him to ask her inside. When he showed no inclination to do so, she said, "Well, Grandpa perked up so much since the last time you were over that I…that we, thought maybe you'd like to come over for dinner and play cards. I got this card game last Christmas that's supposed to be quite fun. I thought we could break them out tonight."

He looked down at his bag for a moment. "Well, I had some plans, but I think they can be changed."

Normally she would've told him not to change his plans, but she felt the sooner Dillon heard from Jerry's own lips that he was no threat the better. It irked her to think about it at all. Besides Jerry's big mouth, and he wasn't the only one on the planet with a big mouth, he'd been nothing but kind to her and Grandpa. Especially to Grandpa. And to her he was nothing but friendly. Even now, with her making a special attempt to ask him over, he didn't act like it was anything more than friendship.

"Good, good. Like I said, it really perked Grandpa up the last time."

"I'll not take it to heart," Jerry said with a chuckle. "He perked up because he beat us so badly."

"We'll see you at say, six o'clock?"

"Sure."

She turned to go.

Back at the house, Taylor sat down with Grandpa and told him everything that happened in the tower room the night before, except for the part about Dillon kissing his granddaughter. She also reminded him not to say anything about Dillon being there. She knew Grandpa wouldn't tell anyone, she only repeated it because Dillon told her to, and she wanted to do everything just right.

Taylor handed Grandpa a cup of coffee.

"So, Dillon has his doubts about Jerry, huh?" he asked.

"Afraid so."

"And you think what, Taylor?" he asked, then slowly sipped his coffee.

"I think you know what I think. He just asks a lot of questions, that's the way he converses." She turned from the counter to look at him. "What do you think?"

"I think the older I get I trust people less and less. Everybody has a weird quirk in them. But Jerry seems nice enough. He was only telling me things you should have told me at the start of coming here, dear." He sipped the coffee again, while watching her take in what he'd said.

"Stress is not good for recovery."

"But it wasn't stressful moving into a deteriorating house?"

She turned back around and slammed her fist on the counter. "Everything I've done lately has been for you. In the past, you loved rebuilding houses, so I bought this house for you. Simply to inspire you to live. And I withheld information from you for good reason."

Grandpa sat his coffee down and said solemnly, "If you had tended to what was best for you, we wouldn't be in this fix."

"You are what's best for me! You're my only family. You're everything to me."

"Taylor," Grandpa said softly trying to calm her. "I can't live forever for you. You must come to terms with that. You have to go out and make your own friends and family."

Pup came into the room and slid under the table to Grandpa's feet when Taylor burst into tears. "I don't want you to die. I want you to live, damn it! I'm an orphan without you. Nobody's ever going to love me like you do."

"No, now Taylor, you've been clinging on to me for dear life ever since your parents died and you have to loosen your grip. True you had a terrible loss and at such a young tender age but - "

"I don't want to go through that again," she sobbed and leaned over the counter. "Oh, I hate crying, I hate it."

"You didn't want to cry when you were a child either, but you have to cry it's part of grieving, dear. Then, it's good for us to cry." After a moment he continued, "Taylor, I have lost a child and I have lost a wife and I have lost my parents. If you live long enough it happens to us all, but I think when God closes a door, he opens a window, making life bearable and even joyful at times. Do the things for yourself that you want me to do. Join groups of interest, make friends, get involved with hobbies. Find a reason to live. Oh, Taylor, you are absolutely a beautiful girl, and you will have a chance at a family of your own, I'm sure."

She sobbed again when he said she was beautiful, the word she wanted Dillon to say last night. Her grandfather never seemed to fail her.

As her tears started to dry, she thought of the irony of it all. She'd talked to a doctor to find out what to do about Grandpa's life and here Grandpa was telling her to do the same with her own.

Turning slowly back around she said to Grandpa, "All right, I pledge to you right now that I will practice the things that you said."

"And I pledge the same to you, Granddaughter."

Taylor noticed rain out the kitchen window and turned with a sigh. She'd hoped to finish painting the house today, but now needed to find something else to do. It was probably not a good idea for her to spend too much time with Dillon in the tower room.

That didn't keep her from thinking about him though. If she wasn't so young, she'd swear she was having hot flashes. However, she figured she'd wait until after she cleaned the kitchen and three bathrooms to take her cold shower.

When she finished in the kitchen, she passed by the tower room with a can of cleanser in her hand.

"Did I tell you I have a big brother?" Dillon called out from the room.

She smiled and turned in. "Yes, I think you mentioned it. At least you're sticking to your story."

"I'm just a tad bit bored," he said with a stretch. "And I'm sure as hell caught up on my paperwork."

"Would some music help? I have an MP3 player."

"Yeah, guess so. You've been avoiding me, haven't you?"

"Well, I thought you could probably use a break."

He didn't deny it, she thought. After a moment of silence she added, "I...uh...went over to Jerry's and asked him over for cards and dinner tonight."

"Good." Then his eyebrows furrowed. "He doesn't think he has a date with you, does he?"

"No, I emphasized that it was for Grandpa."

"Good," he said again, then looked down at some papers beside him. "I need you to fax some papers for me. Can you?"

"Sure, there's a fax machine at school." She looked down at her can of cleanser, then held it up. "Time to clean the bathrooms."

A pop music song came out of MP3 player that she'd plugged into her smart phone. She turned into the bathroom, only having time enough to set the cleanser down before Dillon grabbed her arm and pulled her down the hall and into the tower room. He turned her into his arms and began moving to the beat, his body moves syncing with hers.

"Hey, I need to clean the bathroom," she said with feigned opposition, then laughed.

"You've got time, nothing's growing in there yet."

She closed her eyes and took in the feel of her hand inside his larger one. Her soft palm rubbed against a drier, calloused surface. He squeezed her hand, and she opened her eyes to a smile.

The music changed from upbeat to a slow and sensual song. Dillon had a hand on her waist and one around her hand when they started, but now they released hands. Hers slid to behind his head and his to her hips. He smiled down at her, then leaned down and put his cheek next to hers.

She wasn't going to like it when he moved out of the tower room. The man was a dream. She only changed her mind, slightly, when he hummed off key in her ear.

The rhythm picked up and Dillon waltzed her down the hall, adding an occasional dip here and there. She laughed aloud when he dipped her so far, her hair touched the floor. Later, during an extra-long drum roll, he stopped and looked up at the ceiling. "How are we supposed to dance to that?" He hopped around in what resembled a Native American dance, then stopped abruptly. "Casper won't like that. We better stop."

"What do you mean *we?*" She continued to laugh. He scooped her up in an embrace, then dipped her low again. "Oh, I love you, Dillon. I just love you," she said with joy in her voice.

His jaw flew open, she backed away from him, and covered her mouth.

"Oh. Well." He turned from her and pushed his hair back with a hand. "How about I pay for a couple of pizzas for dinner. That'll make it easier for you."

"Uh...pizza would be nice," she said, rubbing the palms of her hands down the sides of her jeans.

He took some bills from a money clip, put them in her hand, and she put them in her pocket.

The silence was deafening.

"Thanks for the dance," she said and started her work.

———

JERRY ARRIVED AT THE BACK DOOR RIGHT AT SIX. HE CLEANED UP nice. Along with jeans, he wore a new plaid flannel shirt; open, over a crisp T-shirt in a matching color.

Grandpa shook his hand and guided him to the dining room table. Besides being a natural place for Taylor to serve guests, she knew Dillon could hear them from here. Dillon perched on a stool in the hall at Grandpa's bedroom door.

Grandpa, wearing a blue Levi shirt and black jeans, had color in his cheeks. When Taylor went to pick up the pizza, he'd grabbed the plates and forks and put beer and glasses on the table.

Even though Trillium Falls was a small town, it did have an excellent little pizza parlor just out of the city limits. The men stacked their plates with hot pizza and settled down to eat and talk.

"You look good, Gilby. You look well."

Taylor spent extra time on her hair, she sported a stunning new lipstick and tight jeans, but Jerry didn't seem to notice.

"Well, thank you," Grandpa returned.

"Like you don't have a care in the world. So, things must be going well for you here, huh?" Jerry asked as he reached for his plate.

"Oh, everybody starts to look good after they've rested awhile," replied Grandpa, sloughing it off.

Jerry took a bite of pizza and said out of the side of his mouth, "How do you guys like the house now that you've lived here awhile?"

Taylor shook her head. Jack started his twenty questions. If Dillon wanted to hear Jerry's bad side, then he was in luck. That's when she remembered she didn't get any pizza up to Dillon. She wondered how she could get it to him while it was still hot. It would be the right thing to do, especially since he'd paid for it.

"I said, how do you guys like it here?"

"Oh. Sorry. Mouth full," she said with a smile. "I love this house. It'll be beautiful one day."

"Yeah, in the year 2100," Grandpa said sarcastically.

"Well, you guys are getting some things done, aren't you? I mean, I saw the turret room light on one-night last week. You must be doing something in there, huh?"

Grandpa and Taylor exchanged glances. Giving herself time to formulate an answer, Taylor pretended her mouth was full by holding up a hand to her mouth. "Oh, you must mean the tower room."

"Yes. The tower room."

"Well..." She took another bite and looked at Grandpa to help her. He only raised his eyebrows in question at her.

"Don't you think the tower room would be a nice place to sit and read, or just sit and look out over the city?" she asked.

"I've not seen it."

"Oh, of course not."

Jerry tilted his head as if he'd not heard her right, or he was judging her intelligence. "So, what are you doing up there?"

"Only some cleaning." The only thing she'd cleaned up was the floor, with the sleeping bag she and Dillon rolled around in.

"That's all?"

"Yes. We don't quite know how we want to decorate the room."

Grandpa opened his mouth to say something, then closed it, then opened it again. "I'm really not up to fixing the room yet. And Taylor is so busy with work."

"I'll have more time in the summer," she added.

Jerry studied his pizza for a moment and then said, "You suppose I could have a tour of the place?"

"Taylor's got a bunch of laundry all strewn out across the upstairs and the bathrooms are a mess. Perhaps when it's in better shape. It's too embarrassing to take you up there now. Taylor's talents don't lie in housekeeping, I'm afraid."

Taylor stared daggers at her grandfather, while Jerry looked around the room. "Doesn't look too bad on this floor."

"Thanks for your vote of confidence, Jerry," she said with a smile and a pat to his hand.

"That's because I hounded her all day to clean it up," Grandpa replied.

Taylor heard a whimper from Pup, upstairs where Dillon had wanted to keep him. He felt the dog would give him away going back and forth on the stairs.

"Is that your dog?" Jerry asked.

"Yes," she said. "I didn't want him to jump on you, so I put him up in my room."

"Oh, I don't mind the dog," he said and looked at Grandpa.

"I do," Grandpa said, then took another bite.

"Can I use your restroom before we start the cards?"

"Sure, if you can stand the mess," she said and frowned at Grandpa.

Jerry pushed his empty plate back and stood up. He started for the stairs, but Grandpa stopped him saying the clean one was downstairs. Jerry looked up the stairs before he turned to use the bathroom on the main level.

Taylor's thoughts went to getting Dillon some pizza and a rawhide bone to Pup before Jerry made it back to the table. She flew up the stairs and sat back down just as Jerry made his way back.

"You eat a lot for a girl," Jerry said looking at the empty pizza platter. He picked up the cards and began to read the package.

Grandpa slapped his hand on the table. "I'll say. One time she ate so much - "

"That's enough, Grandpa." She knew he was only trying to cover for what really happened to the pizza, but this kind of help she could do without. She wondered why his humor had to be at her expense. Not only was she untidy but now she was a pig, too. Maybe tomorrow it would be funny, she thought, but not right now.

Taylor shuffled the cards, counted out three piles, put the remaining stack in the middle and turned over the top card. "How's your job going, Jerry?"

"Huh? Oh, my job. Won't make me rich."

"Just like a teacher's job, Jerry," said Grandpa. "Taylor tells me you work out at a gym. Didn't know there was one around here."

"It's at the edge of Boise," he answered, not looking up.

"You must be dedicated to travel that far," Taylor said, but thought he didn't have a muscle to prove it. "The object of this game is to use your cards up. You can start one of the four piles with one of these," she said and pointed. "I'll start. Pass."

"Pass," said Grandpa.

"Got to lay a card down here, Grandpa."

Jerry put down a one, then a two and a three. "There's a few around here who make the trip. That Nash guy who used to own this house used to make the trip."

"Oh, you seen him there?" asked Grandpa.

"No, one of the female patrons told me. You guys seen him lately?"

"I saw him a short while ago. He donated some computers to the school," said Taylor.

"Smart public relations move. He won't be around this town long. Guess he's out of town now."

Grandpa looked at Taylor but replied to Jerry. "Oh, is that what they say at the gym?"

"No, a guy he works with said he went to California. Makes a lot of trips down south because he's got a woman there."

How clever of Dillon, she thought, to use that excuse to cover for where he was right now. Yet, the thought of him having a lover pulled at the strings of her heart. She put her head into her hands, rubbed her face and tried to focus on the game.

She succeeded. She played the cards and answered the questions. Now Jerry stood up to leave and they walked him to the door.

When the door closed, she turned to Grandpa. "Do you think he's the one trying to scare us off?"

He sighed. "I'll keep my thoughts to myself tonight, Taylor. I'm pretty tired."

She felt as tired as he looked. She kissed him goodnight and moved ahead of him up the stairs. She turned in at the door leading to the tower room.

"Well, what do you think?" she asked Dillon with a yawn.

"I think he wants up in this room pretty badly."

Taking a defensive stance, she crossed her arms. "And what makes you think that?"

"Weren't you listening to anything he said down there?"

"Yes, I heard you had a girl down south."

"Taylor, you're tired. We'll get to that later. Right now, back to Jerry, he wanted to know what was going on up here. Remember when he asked about the light being on?"

"Yeah, but I suppose half the town could see the light if they looked out their window."

"How about when he asked for a tour?"

"*I* would ask for a tour in a house like this."

"Okay, how about his trying to come upstairs to go to the bathroom."

"It's the first time I know of that he used our bathroom. Grandpa would have to clarify that."

Dillon paced and rubbed his five o'clock shadow. She wondered if he took into consideration anything she'd said.

"He asked someone I work with where I was."

"He asks lots of questions. That's his nature."

"So, besides the fact that his beard doesn't match his hair color is there nothing about him that you question?"

Uncrossing her arms, she chuckled. "All right, I do question all these things, but you have to admit that we can assume all we want, but that doesn't mean it's him. We need more evidence."

Dillon sighed and raked a hand through his hair.

"But there's something else," she began again, "I'd bet this haunted house he doesn't work out. I doubt there's a muscle on his skinny body."

"Is that what you call physical evidence, Taylor?"

"Ha. Ha. But, Dillon, Jerry doesn't have a motive for wanting us out of here. Why in God's green earth would he try to do that? Doesn't make sense."

"Unless he's off his rocker."

She shivered at the thought and turning from him, crossed her arms. "I'll never get any sleep if I keep thinking these kinds of thoughts. I'm going to bed."

Keeping her back to him, she began to leave the room feeling that if she looked back, she'd want to stay and repeat what they started last night. She didn't know if she could bear it if he turned her away.

As she lay in bed, all that haunted her was "the girl down south." She believed he'd used that excuse for his employees, but her tired mind made her wonder. Taylor wanted to cuddle with him more than he did, and she wondered if there was another reason to try to keep her at arm's length.

CHAPTER 18

Monday after work, Taylor squeezed through the kitchen door with two boxes. "Hi, Grandpa."

"Hi, Taylor. How were the wee ones today?"

"Oh, a little off. I think there might be a full moon tonight. But since this is my first year, I still love them terribly."

"Hopefully you'll never get over that. What are the boxes for?"

Taylor walked over to the crock-pot and lifted the lid. Still determined to help repay Dillon for his good deeds, she put a pot roast, carrots, and potatoes on to slow cook that morning.

"They're for Calvin. I'm going to go over and see how the packing is going. Thought I'd offer a few boxes."

"He's going to need those boxes because I haven't noticed any others going to and fro."

"Well, maybe these will encourage him to start, and give me a chance to snoop."

He sighed, "I doubt you'll see much but a bunch of empty booze bottles. Besides, he hasn't the strength to pass up a vodka bottle to stay sober enough to hassle us."

"That's likely, I suppose. He's got to move, Grandpa, he's not our responsibility."

TAYLOR KNOCKED UNTIL HER KNUCKLES HURT, BUT STILL CALVIN didn't open the door. After listening for sounds of life, she leaned over and peered into the window. Her grandfather was right, empty liquor bottles sat on the kitchen counter amongst papers, magazines, dirty dishes and pots and pans. She saw no signs of packing, which frustrated her to no end knowing he only had a few days left.

She took her frustrations out on the door, pounding with all her might. Soon she could see Calvin's shadow coming from the bedroom.

"Who is it?" he shouted from his side of the door.

"Taylor Glenn."

He pulled the door open and scowled at her. "What do you want?"

"Good afternoon. I've got some boxes I thought you might need for packing."

"Don't need any boxes," he barked.

"But these are good copy paper boxes with lids, and I can get more at school."

"Don't need any boxes."

He started to close the door, but she stopped it with her hand. "Where are you moving to, Calvin?"

"That's my business," he said and shut the door in her face.

Taylor shuddered but not from the cold. The sooner he left the better as far as she was concerned. Certainly, the man could understand why she wanted him out. She couldn't afford to have a freeloader. Also, she wondered how much he really did want to stay because he hadn't offered to pay any rent for the place. If he didn't yet understand, he'd learn that in real life you can't expect to be taken care of.

. . .

"I GUESS WHEN THE TIME COMES, WE'LL HAVE TO CALL THE POLICE TO evict him. You can do that you know," said Grandpa as Taylor stirred the beef gravy.

"Yes, but - " The peal of the telephone interrupted her. She walked over to pick up the phone. Hearing nothing but breathing, she hung up and jumped back as if it were a snake.

"I hate that," she said to Grandpa and returned to the stove.

"I don't get calls like that during the day," he said, rubbing his chin.

Ten minutes later, she got another call. Determined she wasn't going to answer any more calls tonight, she let her answering machine get it.

"Oh great, another good meal. Thanks Taylor," said Dillon.

"You're quite welcome, it's the least I can do," she said and handed him a plate of food.

"I see you've got a shadow. Looking for a handout, Pup? Who called?"

She took her own plate from the tray, sat across from him, and pushed Pup's nose away. "Our hang-up caller. But tonight, he decided to deep breathe."

"Damn!"

She put a bite of roast beef in her mouth. "Listen, I stopped by to see Calvin with a few boxes I conveniently thought he might need. You know since he's moving and all. But after a look in his window, I'd say he doesn't plan to leave."

"Maybe he's got a transfer company coming in to move him," he said with a wink.

"Yeah, right."

"Well, was he glad to get the boxes?" he asked, then gave Pup a small piece of fat.

She took a moment to chew and swallow before she began

again. "Absolutely not, he was pretty mad when he opened the door. You would have thought I was peddling religion door to door."

"You said from the window. Didn't he let you in?"

"No, but I had time to peek in the window because it took him awhile to get to the door. Then he tells me, in so many words, to mind my own business."

"Do you think he's mad enough to make the calls?"

She stopped eating a moment, using her full effort to remember when the other calls were made. "Gosh, how should I know? Possibly. I don't think any of the calls were made too late."

"Are you thinking that because of his drinking problem, the calls wouldn't be from him?"

"That's what I think, yes. I'm pretty sure Grandpa thinks so, too," she said a little defensively.

Dillon laid his fork down then stretched his hand out to her in an effort to calm. "But think for a moment what it would be like to lose your home, your place of *free* residence and not much of an income to provide you with another. Would that be cause enough to do what you could to stay?"

Taylor heard the phone ring again. "You mean enough to put aside a drink to be sober enough to mess with the lights? Things like that?"

"Things like that."

She nodded, understanding. "He does have motive. Oh, I can't wait for him to be out of there."

"Expect a little more trouble before it's all over."

Again, she was thankful for Dillon's presence, and she said as much. "What will you be doing when all this is over?"

"The resort here in Trillium Falls is running smoothly which means I don't need to be here all the time."

"What's your next project?"

"There's some riverfront property I want to look at in

Eastern Idaho. I'm thinking of purchasing the property then splitting it up and reselling it with a clause that says a certain construction company must do the building. Then I'll win both ways, you see."

"Are you going home to California first?"

"No."

Taylor was glad about that. But she quickly came to realize, if he wasn't in California, he'd be somewhere else. Somewhere where *she* wasn't. She set down leftover scraps for Pup, then pulled her knees to her chin and let melancholy seep in. "I'll miss you when you're gone, Dillon."

Their gaze held for several moments before Dillon looked away. "You know, I've been working on some computer landscaping today."

"Oh, for the falls project?"

"No, for this house." He picked up his laptop and moved the cursor around. "Come here and look," he said and patted the sleeping bag for her to sit next to him.

She was surprised to see a drawing of her house, then the landscaping appeared. "How'd you do this?" she asked, pleased.

"Technology. I put in the measurements of the house and property."

"Wow, it looks so much better with the landscaping like that."

"Well, I don't think landscaping was necessarily Calvin's gift, you know? I mean he had roses and pansies and such but look what's done here."

"I love the hedges and how they curve around. Can I get a copy of this? Maybe I can do some of this piece by piece."

"Sure, it also lists the descriptions of the plants and how to care for them, plus other tips."

"I can't believe how plants can change the look of the whole place. This is not a picture of a haunted house."

"No, it's not." He turned to the computer again and brought

forth the house with a sign designating it a restaurant. "This is what I was going to do with it."

"Then you found out the history of the house and wondered how you could make a business go without any customers, right?"

He nodded. I bought the house after the owner, Shirley Wilson died of a heart attack. So, it's said anyway."

"And you didn't see anything strange about that. I wouldn't have either. So, probably the worst business mistake you ever made, right?"

"Bull's eye."

"Well, without this house I never would have gotten to meet you," she said and patted his knee. When he didn't say anything, she tried not to let it bother her. Instead, she looked away and noticed some drawings on a yellow tablet. She picked them up. "What's this?"

"Oh, I was only doodling. Making improvements to the house."

"This house?"

DILLON NODDED, PLEASED AT THE EAR-TO-EAR GRIN ON TAYLOR'S face. Her hair fell over her shoulder, and he pushed it back so that he could observe her face as she took in a completely revamped kitchen with an island in the middle and cupboards that reached the tall ceiling. At this moment he was glad his investment had failed.

Somewhere in his chest, he could feel his enjoyable mood move to contentment. He wanted to say the words that echoed through his head. *I want to keep you.*

He tapped the screen with a finger and instead said, "I think the cupboards should be painted white. They should have a window in them showing either the contents or curtains."

"I can picture an island in the middle. This is great. Can I have a copy of this, too?"

"Sure."

She fingered through the other pages. "You're really talented, Dillon. You not only pick the property, but you have an eye for planning out how the whole thing should look, too. And then there's the resort. You should be proud of all you've accomplished at your young age."

If he was a peacock his tail feathers would be showing. "Thank you, ma'am."

Grandpa appeared at the door of the tower room. "Can I come in?"

DILLON WAVED HIM IN. WHEN GRANDPA STOOD BEFORE THEM, Taylor could see something was wrong. Even though the light was fading as the day turned into night, she noted his frown and creased brow.

"Are you okay, Grandpa?"

"No, I'm not okay."

Concerned, Taylor started to get up, but Grandpa put out a hand to stop her. "Sit still, I'm not sick or hurt or anything. I have a confession to make, that's all."

He looked uncomfortable and Taylor's heart beat with foreboding of what was to come.

"Dillon, I'm freeing you. You can go get on with your life and forget about us."

"And what do you know that I don't, Gilby?"

"You don't need to put your life on hold for a few phone calls and lights that flash on and off. And as far as King's going missing goes, we are keeping close tabs on Pup. Not to worry there."

"But it's more than that, Grandpa, your life was threatened. You could have died. You could be pushed again. Or likewise, I could be attacked."

"I won't be attacked, and neither will you."

Dillon rubbed his hand through his hair, repeatedly. "I'm glad you're optimistic, Gilby, but it did happen before."

Grandpa leaned against the wall. "That's just it. I wasn't pushed. There I said it."

"What do you mean you weren't pushed?" Taylor's voice ended in a squeak.

Dillon laid a hand on her knee and shook it. "Let him finish, Taylor."

"I was depressed if that can justify it. I slipped and fell down the stairs. If I told you, Taylor, you'd take time off from work to hold my hand and make sure it didn't happen again. And if you took that much time off from your job, being a first-year teacher and all, you'd likely lose it."

"But, Grandpa - " She felt Dillon's hand again.

Grandpa looked off in space and spoke of Taylor as if she wasn't even there. "If she could believe that someone else had done it and I had used Jerry's ghost stories to make my case, then the attention would be off me. Then Dillon came around and I thought maybe the two of you could become more than friends. Taylor's not in any hurry to settle down so I wanted to make things happen for her."

Surely, her ears had deceived her. It disturbed her to think that he would lie about this. And it seemed strange to her that he'd think that she and Dillon were even friends back then because they really weren't. At that point, they argued most of the time.

If Dillon hadn't already concluded that they were a few cards short of a full deck, he'd believe it now. She looked at Dillon. He patted his knee with the palm of his hand.

"And," Gilby began again, "I didn't know that anything else was going on here. Taylor hadn't told me about the lights or the problems with the door. I thought I was off scot-free. But now, Dillon, you're involved again. It's not right that you're pulled away from your work, and your personal life, for nothing. I'm terribly sorry.

This matter has been gnawing at me for the last few days, ever since Taylor told me everything, and the guilt is killing me because I've not been honest."

Not telling Grandpa about the tower room caused her nothing but problems and she deeply regretted it now. In addition, she was embarrassed for two reasons. First, that Dillon sat there for nothing, and second that Grandpa played matchmaker and now Dillon knew.

As far as Grandpa was concerned, she just wanted to cry. Standing there, he looked one hundred years old. One hundred years accumulated over the last year from the loss of his wife, his illness, and then leaving his home to live here. To live in a place, she expected him to rebuild without an ounce of energy to his name. And to keep his granddaughter from losing the job she planned on for so long, he lied.

"I feel like I can't apologize enough, Dillon," Grandpa said. "We've bungled up our lives badly. It's time for you to be codependent no more. Now it's clear, there's not enough happening around here for you to stay."

Dillon didn't laugh, or cry, or stomp his feet in anger. He looked back and forth from Grandpa to Taylor, his mouth open the whole time. She would say dumbfounded was what he felt. He stood up and absently brushed at the seat of his pants.

"This house has been nothing but bad luck since the first day I saw it," he said shaking his head. "I'll get my stuff and clear out."

Taylor helped him gather his belongings while Dillon rolled up the sleeping bags. "I don't know why you're being so meticulous about these bags; I'm going to have them cleaned anyway," she said trying to make conversation.

He stood up. "Well thanks for the good food. I guess this is goodbye." He stuck out his hand and she shook it, eyes closed, memorizing the feel of it.

"Goodbye, Dillon."

CHAPTER 19

*I*t was a beautiful spring day and a time of new beginnings. Today Taylor strove to forget Dillon, and the house for that matter, as she took Grandpa to Trillium Falls.

Whether confession was good for the soul she didn't know, but Grandpa's health had improved. The day after Dillon left, Grandpa got out and cut the grass. It reminded her of the good old days when she would see him outside working in the yard. The only sign of fatigue that Taylor could see was that he fell asleep an hour earlier than usual.

"What is it you want out of life, Taylor?" he asked while they walked hand in hand along the Trillium Falls trails.

"Oh, for you to be healthy, Grandpa."

"Thank you, Granddaughter, but that's a given. What else?"

"Well, I don't necessarily need to win the lottery, but I'd like to see the house redone, you know. Wouldn't it be grand?"

Grandpa nodded.

"It's the kind of place where you'd never have to move again because it's big enough for, for, anything. Dillon has this neat computer landscaping program where he put in the measurements of our house and yard, then added some ideas of his own, and what he came up with was landscaping that completely changed the look of the place. Anyway, I hope he sends me a copy of it, he said he would, then we could start on the yard. Slowly of course, as we can afford it."

"I'd like to get out and do some yard work again."

"I'd sure like to help you," she returned and squeezed his hand.

"Well, I'm proud of all you've done so far. Sorry I doubted your abilities."

"Apology accepted. Hey, I can't live like a princess forever, you know."

After a nod from Grandpa and a few moments of walking quietly, he said, "Is there anything else you want out of life?"

She took a moment to think about the question. She wanted Dillon, but she also knew that wanting and having were two different things.

"If you want me to say that I want a husband and family then I'll admit to it. Someday. Right now, I am content with wanting our lives to get back to normal, for Calvin to move, and be able to keep my teaching job amid budget cuts. Then after work and during the summers I have off, I can fiddle with the house. When things settle, I'll try to make friends and be open for dating. When things settle."

"Well, at least you said it, Taylor, that you'd like a family other than me."

Yes, she said it, but Dillon made her think it. Even for those few days, she enjoyed coming home and seeing him, talking with him, and kissing him.

"I hope I didn't scare Dillon off," said Grandpa with a frown.

"No, I don't think so. Dillon has a whole other life out there without us. He was charitable enough to lend us a helping hand when we needed it."

"You think he thought of us as a charity?"

"It's a good way to think of it, that way feelings aren't hurt," she said.

"I see."

Grandpa didn't see. How could she ever pass by the tower room and not think of Dillon? How could she ever hear she ever hear that song again and not think of the way Dillon danced and whirled her around the room? And she hoped she would experience once again, in her lifetime, the kind of physical heat that emanated when they came together.

Dillon had shown up every time she needed him and put a roof on her house when no one else wanted to. He sincerely hoped his electronic contributions to the school district would help save her job. He was her helper, friend and could've probably been more. She had loved and lost but she would not cry today.

To prevent her from doing so, she took a deep breath of the fresh air and tried to concentrate on the beauty of the nature around her. Grandpa walked at a leisurely pace holding the handrail that someone painstakingly provided. They came across the first waterfall and walked under it feeling the light spray of water on their faces.

"And what about you, Grandpa, what do you want out of life? Turnabout is fair play," she said with a smile when he looked at her.

"I, too, want my health back of course, and where my health is concerned, I can finally see the light at the end of the tunnel and it's not a train," he said, his breathing slightly labored from the effort of both walking the bumpy path and talking. "For a while there, I thought I would be useless forever, so I'd be extremely happy to putter around the house and yard working on this and that. It all adds up, you know. Yes, that would suit me just fine."

Maybe it wasn't such a bad mistake to buy this house after all, she finally, fully believed.

"I don't want to do any cooking."

She laughed in response. "I suppose I can suffer through the cooking."

With a breath, he added, "And I want to do a few things for others, too. Maybe I can start by coming to school one day a week and help some kids with reading."

"Wow, that's great."

"Don't get too excited. It'll be a while before I get the kind of energy I need to wrestle school children."

She knew he said that to cover his self-consciousness.

"And I've been waiting all my life to join one of those senior groups that take all those little trips here and there and see everything."

"Sounds like a perfect life to me, Grandpa."

"Not quite, I want great grandchildren."

"Someday, Grandpa, some day." She took another gulp of air and proceeded down the trail.

———

TODAY CALVIN SWEENEY HAD TO VACATE THE PREMISES. IT WAS A Friday and a workday for Taylor, so Grandpa was going to watch for any kind of movement, until after work when she would stand vigil. They decided they wouldn't push him today. Tomorrow, they would go to Calvin and demand he leave the apartment. She wanted Calvin to think they'd involve the police.

When she arrived home from work nothing was different, still no sign of moving. Taylor busied herself with laundry trying to keep her mind off what they would say and do tomorrow.

Later, she looked up from washing dishes and spotted Jerry heading their way. Which didn't surprise her, she knew he wanted the lowdown on Calvin. She could hear the questions now, "Did he move? When will he? Where's he going to go? Are you going to call the police?"

Maybe tonight she would tell him to mind his own business, or maybe not, because a game of cards would be a good way to keep her mind off this mess.

———

"Jerry, I like you, but you ask too many questions. Some things we like to keep to ourselves, and Calvin is one of them. Can we just play cards?"

Jerry stood abruptly. "Friends ask questions. Conversations are made up of questions and answers. I might ask too many questions, but you're a tight-lipped... Who thinks if she so much as mentions the brand name of her toothpaste the Russians will get wind of it and set off the third world war."

"Here, here," said Grandpa to both.

Jerry departed in anger, leaving Taylor with a game of fifty-two-card pick up.

That night the lights went on and off in the tower room, the dog barked, and the phone rang but it didn't really bother Taylor like it used to. It also helped her to sit in the tower room with Dillon. It somewhat desensitized her fear of the room.

Yet, because of the dog barking and the telephone ringing, her sleep was broken. She woke up tired and disturbed that they had lost Jerry as a friend. Grandpa didn't deserve to lose Jerry's friendship. She decided she would apologize as soon as this affair with Calvin was over, besides, then she would have something to tell him.

Again, they watched out their kitchen window for signs of moving. Nothing. In procrastination, she waited until four o'clock.

"Go away!" shouted Calvin on the other side of the door. "I'm not moving!"

Grandpa and Taylor exchanged glances, then Grandpa said, "Looks like it's going to have to be the police, Taylor."

"You will move, or we'll have the police move you!" she shouted back.

No response.

She'd give him a little time to ponder their threat. Which she knew was silly because he wasn't using his time tonight to pack.

She wondered what her other options were. She thought maybe she could go in when he was out and change the locks. No, she decided, that was dumb because she would be stuck with all his stuff. Not to mention that it was probably a crime, too.

Around eight o'clock, she passed by the tower room with folded laundry in her arms and saw, probably for the one-hundredth time, the tower room door open and the light on. She let out an audible sigh and shook her head, but on the way back downstairs she noticed the light was off.

Something seemed to snap in her and she took the stairs two at a time. She angrily stomped through the dining room then into the kitchen where she grabbed her keys.

Grasping the ring, she left the house and pounded on Calvin's door. Just as she anticipated, no reply. She also expected to see a passed out drunk, either on the couch or in his bed, but she found neither. She was alone, which was good because she was determined to find where the electrical problem in the tower room originated. Or learn she had a ghost.

Taylor wondered briefly where Calvin could be, but her anger didn't allow her to care. She looked around the small apartment trying to envision where she was in proportion to what was on the other side of the wall. One thing she already knew and that was that the apartment was on the ground floor and the tower room was upstairs.

She left the apartment door open and flew back to her kitchen to get a flashlight, then went around the outside of the house and shone the light up to where the tower room was and tried to figure out where they were in proximity to Calvin.

If not mistaken, there was a space between them that was unaccounted for. She had not noticed it before mainly because she'd only seen Calvin's apartment once or twice and then briefly. And this was a *big* house.

When she made her way back to Calvin's, the door was shut and locked. Thankful she still had her keys, she decided to call it a night. She would talk this over with Grandpa and they would come here tomorrow, Calvin or no Calvin, and they would find out what made up that space.

———

AFTER BREAKFAST THE FOLLOWING DAY, TAYLOR TOOK GRANDPA around to the side of the house. After talking about the rooms on each floor, she added, "So there has to be a space between Calvin's apartment and the tower room, see?" said Taylor and pointed upward.

"I see," he said and rubbed the stubble on his chin. "Taylor, we need to call the police and get Calvin out of here."

"Just give me a little more time, okay Grandpa? This is important to me."

"I don't know," he answered as he looked back up to the tower room. "Where do you think the entry point is? I mean from the apartment to the tower room."

"I'm thinking it has to be from the bedroom," she said, biting at her thumbnail. "Maybe from the closet."

"Or maybe a panel in the wall. So, what's your next plan, Taylor?"

"I'm going to say a prayer then knock on the door and try to talk sense into him. Probably not unlike the way I talk to my first graders."

"Well, good luck. I'm going to work on the lawnmower. See if I can squeeze a little more life out of it."

After Taylor put the breakfast dishes in the dishwasher, she took Pup out to the backyard. She stared at the apartment while Pup watered the bushes and concluded that Calvin wasn't home. The usual daytime signs of Calvin's presence, such as lights and the television blaring, were not present. She pounded on the door with her fist, then listened.

Her heart picked up a beat, so she looked down and let out the breath she'd been holding, then reminded herself she had a right to go into the apartment. She took the keys, unlocked the door and crept in.

"Calvin? Calvin!" When she didn't receive an answer, she walked back to the bedroom and started looking for a closet, bookcase, or panel. After looking back toward the door for any signs of Calvin, she slowly opened the closet and peered inside. So, he had been packing because there wasn't anything inside. At least he had the closet stuff packed.

Again, she took a quick look behind her, stepped into the closet and did indeed find something. A locked door. She hurriedly tried each key on her ring and found that the key to the apartment also fit into this door.

The situation was unsettling to say the least and she wondered if she should go back and get Grandpa, but then decided she didn't have time for that as Calvin could be back at any moment. Besides, she only needed a little peek into this door.

Heartbeats pounded in her chest. Still, she opened the door slowly, standing back, barely peeking around. The room was dark, so she reached for a light switch on the inside wall and found one.

Steps led up to an empty room with another door at the far side of it. Stepping inside, she ventured up, then over to the other door after the first door shut with a resounding boom, and what sounded like the click of a prison cell door.

Taylor touched the keys in her pocket for reassurance then worried when she saw, on closer examination, that the doorknob didn't have a keyhole.

"Calvin?"

No answer.

She started pounding on the door. "Calvin! This is not funny! Let me out!"

"Damned woman! Why should I let you out when you're trespassing!" Calvin returned, just as angry.

"But I'm not! You were supposed to be out day before yesterday. You weren't home so I came in to see if you'd moved."

"This is my home! And now you've broken in."

She hammered the door with her fist again. "I'm sorry that you can't live here, Calvin, but this is my home now. I can't afford to have you here any longer. You have to find another place."

"Easy for you to say on the other side of this door."

Turning, she looked around the room. There was no way out except, perhaps, through the other door. She turned the knob and found it locked. With shaking hands, she tried every key, finding no match.

She feared Calvin had left her there alone, and the silence was deafening. After walking back to the door connecting to the closet, she looked closely at the handle to see if there was any way she could loosen the handle with the keys she held in her hand. There were two small screws on either side of the handle. The screws looked too small to take out with her keys.

"Calvin!"

"What?!"

Relieved he was still there, she let out a breath. "Let me out and we can talk this over face to face."

"My problem is solved because no one will find you."

Taylor almost mentioned Grandpa but hesitated because Calvin could do something to him. She hoped she could pull off a lie. "Calvin, I've hired a lawyer and he knows you won't move out. I'm a young healthy woman so if something happens to me you will be a suspect."

"You might be young and healthy, but your grandfather isn't."

Now her horror intensified. Was he drunk or was he crazy? She didn't have enough experience with either to know the difference.

"Please Calvin, if it means that much to you, of course you can live here. I love what you've done with the roses and some of the other plants."

"Ha! You don't even know what those plants are called. That's how much you pay attention to what I do around here. Didn't thank me for boarding up that window either."

"Well, I'm thanking you now. If I'd known it was you, I would have thanked you right away. Please Calvin, let me out."

"I think you need to stay there so you'll never bother me again."

Oh, she was sorry she hadn't heeded Grandpa's advice and called the police. Now she wondered if she was going to die in this place. She backed up against the wall, slid down to sit on the floor, and started to cry when she wondered what her little first graders would do without her.

Standing up, she wiped her tears and ran with all her might, slamming her shoulder into the door. When the only damage done was to her shoulder, she kicked and kicked making only small dents in the sturdy door.

She had to think, she had to think! If only she could invent something that would make Calvin think she'd be found. "Dillon... Dillon will come looking for me!" she shouted with a sob. "And once my dog gets my scent or hears my noise, it will be easy for Dillon to find me."

"What? You think that dog's Lassie or something?" He guffawed. "That dog will be just as easy to make disappear as the last one. And you can take the blame for that because I forewarned you about that big, stupid dog."

"Oh no, oh *no*," she whispered, alarmed over what he had done and what more he could possibly do.

"And Dillon won't come looking for you. He wouldn't want a schoolmarm when he could have some rich bimbo. Good looking man like that should add to his fortune with a rich woman. That's what I'd do, yes ma'am."

Even though she doubted Calvin's reasons, he was right about Dillon not coming back. Yet, she couldn't think about her loss now because she had Grandpa to worry about and her dog as well.

It had come to this. She wiped tears from her eyes and wondered if she'd ever get a chance to say near enough how sorry she was for buying this house in the first place. She needed Grandpa to hear her say it with her whole heart before something fatal happened to them.

Taylor heard a door shut in the distance then a horrible wave of silence engulfed the room once more. She worried that maybe Calvin had gone off to find Grandpa. With unsteady hands, she grabbed her keys and started working on the door hinge. She poked and jabbed and tried to twist to no avail. Then she sat on the floor and worked at the tiny screws beside the handle.

When one screw moved slightly, she tried the other and it too moved slowly but surely. Finally, her hands started to steady, and her forehead and shirt became wet from perspiration.

After what seemed liked hours, she got the screws out and the handle off. She found that the doorknob on the other side could completely come apart, so she worked at it until she got the door open.

Wasting no time, she ran to the kitchen and called 911, then grabbed the downstairs baseball bat and looked for her grandfather.

The backdoor opened and Taylor turned, ready to strike the intruder. When she saw it was Grandpa, she shook uncontrollably.

"You look like you've seen a ghost. What's the matter? Your hand's bleeding."

She looked down at her trembling hand. She hadn't realized she'd hurt her fingers trying to get the door open. Then her eyes flashed behind him to the hallway. Afraid Calvin could be in the house, she led Grandpa out and onto the driveway where they waited for the police.

"Calvin wasn't home, so I went into the apartment and found the entryway we've been after."

"Why'd you go in there? You should've waited," said a perturbed Grandpa.

"I know. I was wrong, very wrong. Calvin shut me in a room and then left. I had to take the doorknob apart to get out. Not only that, but he also admitted to getting rid of King, and boarding up the window. He must've climbed in the window from the deck, which was quite a stretch. Bad back, my foot."

Her eyes continued to scan the area until the police arrived. Then she burst out in tears of relief.

When two men in blue got out of their car, she told them about the date of eviction for Calvin and explained all that happened to her since.

"Does this information have to go to the newspaper?" she asked. "I'd like to staunch any gossip about my house."

"It's going to be hard to keep this quiet, ma'am, if you're going to press charges. Then it will have to go to trial."

"I just want him out of here. And his stuff."

Both men looked up at the house, the tower room to be more specific, and then at each other. "Ma'am, if we can find him, we'll take him in overnight and release him in the morning. That'll give you enough time to move his stuff out to storage and change the locks. Bring the storage information to the jail and we'll give it to him when we let him go."

"Yes, I like that. That will be good, right Grandpa?"

Grandpa rubbed his chin, "Yes."

Upon agreement, the police officers went into Calvin's apartment while she and Grandpa waited in the driveway. When they came out, they inspected the yard, spoke quietly, and went separate ways. They walked a circle in the yard until one sprung over Jerry's wooden fence and grabbed Calvin up by the arm.

Relieved, Taylor and Grandpa went in the house where Grandpa started a pot of coffee. "We're going to need this if we've got a move ahead of us tonight."

Taylor sat at the table and put her head on her arms. The fear of being locked in a room left her emotionally and mentally drained. However, all she could do now was feel sorry for an old man who had no place to go. It took her a few moments to realize that it wasn't her job to see that Calvin had a place to live. He could do that for himself.

"I wonder why Dillon didn't try to help Calvin like he helped us," Grandpa asked, looking out the window.

"That's a good question. I don't know, Grandpa."

"Yeah, he was an old man same as me. Well, too late to ponder that now, let's get moving. Literally."

CHAPTER 20

*T*aylor and Grandpa worked until one o'clock in the morning getting Calvin's possessions into storage. Luckily, his personal effects were limited, but she found it strange that the kitchen cupboards were bare. Didn't the man insist on staying? Everything that was on the counter was all he had in the kitchen.

With the job done and the locks changed, she got Grandpa home to bed and took the storage key to the Trillium Falls Police Department.

On the way home, she sang along with the radio, giddy with joy and relief. Then later, even though her sleep was cut short, she sang on her way to work.

Interested in keeping a friendship going with Johnna, she stopped by the nurse's room to tell her about the weekend. "To make a long story short, I think Calvin was the one trying to scare us out and I'm so relieved he's gone."

"Wow, he actually shut you up in a room?" asked Johnna with a shiver.

Taylor nodded.

"He sounds nuts. He won't come back, will he?"

"I don't think so, because the police told me that if he harasses us again, he will do jail time."

"How is that?"

"We filed a restraining order; he's not to come around. Then there's breaking and entering if he chooses to do so, and on and on," Taylor said with a wave of her hand. "I doubt he'll be back knowing all that."

"Yeah, I see what you mean. Now maybe your life can get back to normal, huh?"

"What's normal?" Taylor looked up at the clock and grimaced, she had to get ready for her students. She headed for the door.

"Taylor? One more thing. Will you be seeing Dillon again?"

She turned slowly. "No, I don't think so."

"I'm sorry to hear that, dear."

Taylor nodded in response.

———

"How are you feeling today, Grandpa?" Taylor asked, flipping through the mail.

Grandpa rotated his shoulders. "Oh, a few sore muscles, but pretty good, thank goodness."

"Good. All's quiet on the western front?"

"Yes, ma'am."

"Good. Isn't it great that this thing is all over?" Maybe she wouldn't have to express regret for buying the house after all.

"Yes, ma'am. I'm thinking about finishing the painting tomorrow."

"Excellent."

He rotated his shoulders again. "Yeah, I'm not too sore. I should be fine tomorrow."

Taylor laid the mail down. "Grandpa, I think we need to check out the apartment again."

"Sure, I would like to get a better look at it to see what needs to be done to be renter ready. Eventually, of course."

After Calvin, the thought of another renter was repulsive to her, and she'd need time to consider that plan. "I mean we need to see what's on the other side of that door."

"No breaks for you, huh?"

She shook her head.

He sighed. "Okay, after dinner."

"Is that a hint?" she returned with a smile.

"You can take it as such, yes."

They hugged each other soundly.

Taylor said a silent prayer of thanks for Grandpa's good health. Now there was nothing the two of them couldn't do to restore this place and have a good life.

She didn't really need Dillon anymore. Instead of feeling appeased by this, she felt a void inside that wasn't going to be easy to fill. Even though she'd spent relatively little time with him, she felt it would take a long time to forget him.

Dillon made her want now. Besides a grandfather, she wanted a husband, a physical and spiritual relationship with a man that would produce children. She hoped the vision that Dillon inspired in her would be a glimpse of what her future would hold.

"THE PLACE NEEDS A GOOD CLEANING," GRANDPA OBSERVED AND followed Taylor into the apartment's kitchen.

"Yeah, looks like he didn't do any vacuuming."

"I guess some men don't take it as serious as women do."

"Glad I didn't say that," she shot back with a smile.

Looking around she could see that they needed to put in new

carpet, linoleum, and a few coats of paint. "Lots of fixing up to do in here as well."

"People aren't hiding Jews from Hitler anymore, so what good is a room that you have to get to through a closet? It'll have to be changed." He pushed open the knob-less door, then added, "We could make the apartment larger if we made some changes here."

"How are we going to get through this next door? None of the keys fit."

"Good question, girl. But seems to me you're the expert at taking a doorknob off," he said with a chuckle.

She could laugh about it now because it was all over. "I'd rather use an ax or some tools, Grandpa."

"Let's not use an ax. It's a good door and we can still use it. I'll go get something. Be right back."

Being alone in this room again gave her the chills, so she left to wait in the apartment's kitchen. Before long, Grandpa came back carrying a tool bag and an electric drill.

They both hesitated a moment, exchanging glances and sighs, before they opened the final door. In her mind's eye she'd pictured human bones and her heart picked up a pace. It surprised her when the door swung open to a few more steps and a room glowing with lights.

It was some sort of nursery or greenhouse with artificial lights, hanging over row after row of greenery. The plants had a leaf that fanned out like a hand with one long point in the middle, then coming in smaller points at the side. To Taylor, the plants appeared to be all the same variety, a range of sizes from seedlings to monster plants. A partially filled bucket held pruned leaves.

"What in the world?" asked Grandpa, more to himself than to Taylor.

Taylor spread her fingers out across the lower portion of her face. "It must be marijuana."

"Well, no kidding," Grandpa said sarcastically. "And I don't think it's grown to be used as rope."

"Oh *no*, what are we going to do, Grandpa? We could be put in jail for this."

"Kind of a lot to flush down the toilet."

"But we have three toilets and one here in this apartment."

"There's too much here to flush, I'm afraid."

"Oh no, oh *no*." Their lives had gotten better and now this. Would their troubles never cease? It was like the domino theory, one piece of her life after another toppling down to ruin.

Due to the laws on drug testing, the least she could lose was her job. Forget the drug testing; she owned a whole, large room full of the stuff. That would not set well with the school administrator. Moreover, they'd go to jail.

"If we call the police, would they believe that we didn't do this?" she asked.

Taylor turned with a startled jump when she heard someone at the door. It was Calvin. "Not when I tell them you did. If you would have left well enough alone, I would still be living here, and no one would be the wiser."

Her first thought was that Grandpa must have left the apartment door unlocked when he came back through with the tools. However frightening Calvin's reappearance was, he didn't appear to have a gun so if push came to shove, they could tackle him and tie him up until they got rid of the plants.

With full force, Grandpa started pulling out the plants and dropping them on the floor. "Taylor, never mind that old weasel, start killing these plants."

"Oh no you don't," Calvin bolted over to Grandpa and pushed at him.

Taylor aimed her foot at Calvin's back when she heard another noise behind her. Turning, she prayed it was not the police.

It was Jerry Garcia. "What's going on here?"

Grandpa went back to pulling the plants out, "I'm doing a little weeding. Please help Jerry, seems Calvin's been doing his own kind of gardening."

"Stop, I tell you!" Calvin pushed at him again.

Jerry waved his arms. "Stop everybody, stop! Now! And tell me what's going on."

"Jerry, we haven't time for twenty questions," said Taylor, exasperated at him.

"You will tell me everything and from the beginning," Jerry returned sternly.

Taylor ignored him and went to pulling out the plants herself, until she heard another voice in the room.

"I agree with Jerry. Everybody stop and start talking." It was Dillon and he held a gun on them all.

The gun freaked her out and for a moment she wondered if she was going to pass out. A wave of Dillon's gun encompassed them all and a fear arose within, causing her to wonder if she ever knew him at all. How could she have forgotten about his criminal record? He backed to the wall that linked to the tower room and tried to keep his eyes on them while he examined a switch on the wall. When he flipped the switch up and down and nothing happened, she assumed it was the answer to the tower room light show.

Steeped in fear, she wondered if he could possibly be signaling someone else. She watched him move back, down toward the entrance, and push the door shut.

"Calvin, why are you here?" Dillon asked.

"Because I live here."

"He does not. Grandpa and I moved him out and we have a restraining order on him. He will go to jail."

Calvin turned to look at her and venomously spit out the words, "Yeah, well now who's going to jail?"

"Calvin," Dillon said, "I can see why you didn't take my financial offer to move. This operation would produce far more money than the piddling sum I offered."

Why did Dillon offer Calvin money without telling her? Taylor wondered with dismay.

"I don't know what you're talking about. I chose not to move because this is my home. This operation belongs to them," he pointed to Taylor and Grandpa.

"It does not! And why don't you tell them about your locking me in that, that room."

"You broke into my apartment, and you accidentally locked yourself in. It's as easy as that. To think to blame me." He shook his head with mock sadness on his face.

"Then why do you want me to stop pulling up the plants?" shot in Grandpa.

"Why evidence, of course."

Taylor could see Grandpa's face redden in anger, so she placed herself between Calvin and Grandpa.

"Don't move!" Dillon blasted out and she shrieked. Dillon was brutally cold, and she didn't like it. How could he dare to point a gun at Grandpa, or herself for that matter?

"No, just shoot me and put me out of my misery," she shot back, her voice wobbling with emotion.

Jerry had taken that moment to move, and Dillon swung the gun back to face him. "Take another step and I'll blow a hole through you."

"Okay, okay. Easy."

"Now I want all of you to start pulling up the plants," demanded Dillon.

"No!" shouted Calvin.

"And why not?"

"Because, because this is evidence. I can take care of this after they go to jail."

"The plants are evidence pulled up or not. Pull 'em up, Calvin."

"No!" Calvin pushed at Grandpa as he tried to uproot the plants. Grandpa put a hand on his heart and started breathing heavily.

Taylor didn't care about being shot, she pushed at Calvin so hard he fell over, then Jerry plopped down on top of him. Dillon stepped back and lifted the point of his gun allowing the altercation.

"Ouch, ouch, be careful! That she-devil, she should have died, too!"

"What do you mean, too?" asked Jerry.

Taylor figured Calvin must have realized he said too much because he started moaning, then struggled to get free.

"Was it Shirley? Maybe she didn't want to move either."

It took a moment for the name Shirley to register. Taylor's eyes widened when she realized who Jerry was talking about. "Shirley was the name of the former owner who died of a heart attack."

Calvin's useless struggles ceased, and he tried to turn his head toward Taylor. "You think I'm here to do your damn yard? No way. You think I'm some drunken bum who doesn't even have a place to stay? Ha! You should see my house. *This* is the yard work I do and I'm damn good at it, too."

"I would say so, you've got more than a hundred grand growing right here," said Jerry.

"That's right," Calvin answered, then his eyes narrowed. "How would you know?"

"I might ask you the same question, *Garcia*. What's in this for you? And who are you anyway?" Dillon pointed the gun at Jerry who had a knee on Calvin's back. He started to reach for his back, but Dillon aimed the gun at his head. Jerry quickly put his hands up over his head.

"My name's Jerry Crandall. I'm with the police department, on the drug task force. Seems Calvin's done a little bragging and I happened to get wind of it."

"I'll see your ID. Get it *slowly*."

Dillon checked it, then nodded and lowered his gun.

"And what's in it for you?" Jerry asked Dillon.

"Taylor." He looked at her a moment, and then at the gun. "This is just a pellet gun I found stuck in one of the boxes left in the shed," he said, and Calvin groaned. "I knew there was something more going on in this house. I've kept my distance lately from Gilby and Taylor, but I've been around, covertly waiting for a moment like this.

Taylor, happy with the way the events had transpired, turned to her grandfather. "Are you all right, Grandpa?"

"Sure am."

"But when you put your hand on your heart-"

"Just thought it might deter Calvin is all," he cut in. "Got to use your brain when your brawn is weak. I'm fine."

Taylor turned to Jerry and chuckled. "I'm sorry I gave you such a hard time, but you really were annoying with all the questions."

"Just doing my job, ma'am. Just doing my job," he returned with a smile. He put handcuffs on Calvin, then stood him up. Calvin gnashed his teeth while Jerry read him his rights.

Taylor's gaze went to Dillon and joy filled her soul. When he smiled in return, she ran to him and jumped in his arms. Dillon held her up by the seat and her legs wrapped around his hips. He spun her around as he hugged her, and she felt so…so unfettered that she threw her head back and laughed. It was as if she was intoxicated without putting a single plant aflame.

She was free of the stigma attached to this house now that every stone was unturned. She finally knew that Dillon wanted her and with Grandpa's good health there was nothing more she needed. She was content.

CHAPTER 21

From a kitchen window, Taylor watched Jerry put Calvin into a squad car. She turned to her grandfather. "Not only is he to be charged with drug manufacturing but the case with Shirley Wilson is to be reopened. Jerry said even if he got off scot-free in the Wilson case, he still faced a minimum of ten years in prison for the manufacturing of marijuana."

"And us? Are we held liable in any way because the harvesting was done in our house?" Lines of concern moved deep across Grandpa's brow.

"Jerry said no. He said until tonight, he didn't know who was involved. Of course, he did think Calvin was because of the scuttlebutt he'd heard, but he didn't know if anyone else was involved. When Dillon came back into the picture, he wondered whether his fortune was made by real estate alone. Jerry also had to figure out where the stash was, too."

"I see, I see," said Grandpa.

"Yeah, well we all wondered why Dillon was back."

"And here I thought Jerry was my new best friend," Grandpa said with a chuckle.

"Guess he came to work during the day and watched the place from the neighboring house. Remember when I saw him coming home from the gym? Well, he was just coming to work."

"That's why he didn't have many belongings in the house," said Grandpa.

"Yep."

Taylor heard another vehicle and went to the window. She bit her lip in disappointment.

"Who's that?" asked Grandpa.

"It's Dillon leaving. I was hoping he'd come in and say goodnight."

"Well, it's been quite a night. He's probably tired, as we all are." Grandpa was placating her, she could tell. He stood up, stretched and with a yawn, he said, "Time for bed. It's all over now, we can finally rest."

"True, but what about Dillon?" She hoped her grandfather had an answer for her.

"We'll just have to see, Granddaughter. You've done all you can. Leave it at that."

She nodded and followed him to the stairs. No more than an hour before, she felt like she had the world at her feet but now she wasn't so sure. Dillon had that much effect on her.

———

THE FOLLOWING DAY AFTER WORK, TAYLOR DECIDED TO RETURN TO the scene of the crime. The police department didn't make it out to retrieve the plants, but she was sure it would happen soon.

Taylor looked around the two rooms she hadn't even known she had and tried to figure out what structural changes needed to be made. With a smile, she decided she'd make something positive out of all of this by adding them to the main house. It would be perfect for a nursery and playroom. Then her countenance fell when she thought of Dillon.

She tried to encourage herself by admitting that it was not a bad thing to hope for a husband and a family. Changing these rooms would be like a living marker reminding her of this time and a memento of the fact that she needed to let go of her unrealistic hold on Grandpa.

After shaking her head, she started going through the cupboards in the apartment's kitchen with a spray cleaner and a towel. She groaned. In her rush to move Calvin, she'd overlooked a cupboard. Thankfully, it only contained three liquor bottles. Two bottles of vodka and one of scotch.

Never having had a taste of vodka, she was curious. She unscrewed the top and took a sip, swallowing it gently, careful not to irritate her throat. Yet, she didn't need to be so careful. She unscrewed the next bottle and then the Scotch. All three bottles held water.

So, Calvin wasn't really a drunk. He, like Jerry, lived here only when he worked. How stupid of her to think he couldn't be bothered after the bewitching hour. The Sprite bottle he carried around probably was Sprite. She laughed aloud.

She felt it was a shame you couldn't trust anyone anymore. How could she find a way to teach her first graders not to trust so completely?

When she left the apartment, she spotted Dillon in the driveway. He took a sheet of glass, partially wrapped in cardboard, from the back of his truck. She waited for him at the back porch. Although elated to see him, she put a hand to her chest to push her feelings down, to try and protect herself from wanting too much. Believing he was hers last night, until he left without saying goodbye, caused her to think that she couldn't let herself believe he was anything but a friend.

"Hello. What's going on?"

"How about a window for the tower room in exchange for dinner?" he said with a smile.

When she nodded, he added, "Thought Gilby and I could work on this together."

Grandpa was thrilled at the prospect. In the kitchen, they talked of how they would repair the window and what they needed for the job, while Taylor decided to make hamburgers and homemade fries.

"We kind of thought you were going to come in last night, what happened?" There Grandpa said it and she didn't have to. She grabbed an onion with dual purpose, a condiment for the hamburgers and a reason to cry if she needed one.

"Well, I followed Jerry to the police department. I wanted to see it through. By then it was late, and I didn't want to bother you two."

"Sure, makes sense," said Grandpa.

Taylor laid the chopped onion aside and grabbed a tomato from the refrigerator, not missing the wink Grandpa gave her.

The news nearly put a brick through her wall of protection, but she still told herself to proceed with caution. She needed to have a long talk with Dillon. So many questions remained unanswered, and she needed to finally start being open and upfront, as she should have done with Dillon and Grandpa, from the very beginning.

She waited until they finished the window. Dillon came into the kitchen, where she sat paying bills, and washed his hands and face.

"Dillon, we need to talk."

He turned from the sink and gave her a searching look. "Okay. Come see the window first, looks pretty good."

The improvement was considerable, adding light to the room, and a larger view of the town. Grandpa was proud as a peacock having been involved in the project. He excused himself to turn in early, then Dillon turned to her.

She looked up at him prepared to be serious but couldn't help but return the brilliant smile he gave her. It was hard to keep her mind on what she wanted to say, or ask, when her mind flashed back to his kisses in this very room. Turning from him, she walked to the window and looked out. After taking a breath she said, "I need to know about Kirsten Olson."

He looked at her in question, then with concern on his face. Perhaps a little *too* concerned for her liking. "Why? What's wrong? Did she call here?" He started to head for the door.

"Where are you going?" she asked, flustered.

"To grab my cell." He walked back toward her, his anxiousness heightening. "She did call, didn't she?" he asked again.

She stretched her hand out and patted the air to calm him. "No. She didn't call. Let's start this again. I think that we need to be honest and up front with each other and to start, I'm asking about Kirsten Olson."

"You say Kirsten. Where did you hear that name?" he said with an endearing smile that further confused her.

Taylor reminded herself that she needed to tell the truth and nothing but the truth, no matter what. Looking down at the floor, she said in a quiet voice. "Back when I knew nothing about you, when I had to assume that everyone was guilty until proven innocent, I looked at your computer that first time you stayed here. I saw Kirsten Olson labeled as your beneficiary. I also noticed that she gave you a considerable amount of money at one time."

"What? You logged on to my computer?"

She flinched and then shook her head. "It was already on. I...a bumped it and-"

"Wait, never mind that, you thought I was guilty of something, so instead of being up front with me you snooped?"

She nodded, looking down.

"And why would you be interested in my beneficiary unless you were concerned about my money?"

With a hand up, she said firmly, "First questions, first. Is she a woman you go home to see?"

"This is unbelievable," he said to the ceiling, then paced a few steps and turned toward her. "I'm super tired and now angry. I need a break." Proceeding to leave, he turned at the doorway and said, "Kirsten Olson is my mother, but she goes by KC. Short for Kirsten Cathleen. She has a different last name because she got married some years back. She married into money, so she invested in my company. You don't need to be jealous of her, I'm not into incest."

Thinking back, she thought she heard him call his mother Casey. "Oh, Casey. KC," she said to the empty room.

How foolish she felt. Now she would be surprised if Dillon ever came back. Not only did he think her dishonest by snooping, but now his biggest fear was manifest: she wanted his money. Disheartened, she pulled the tower room door shut and headed for her bedroom. Pup came out of Grandpa's room and followed her down the hall.

"At least I have you," she told the dog and patted his head.

Sitting down on the edge of her bed she spent a few extra minutes petting Pup and made a decision. She had plenty of things to do around here to keep her from stewing over Dillon. Tomorrow morning, she would rent a steamer and get some of the wallpaper off the walls. Thank goodness, she had something to do.

Pup put his front paws on her knees, and she kissed him on the top of his head. "You don't look like a pup anymore. I've got to find you a name."

———

THE FIRST THING SHE NOTICED SATURDAY MORNING WAS THAT THE tower room door was open. She'd talked with Grandpa about keeping the door shut, only heating the areas they used the most. Yesterday, she noticed that it was open too, but she thought that perhaps she'd left it open by mistake. This time she knew without a doubt the door was closed the night before. It surprised her how fast that familiar fear could settle back into her stomach.

"Grandpa, did you open the tower room door this morning?"

"No, not with an electric bill like ours." He was pouring coffee but stopped midstream to look at her. "Why?"

"Are you sure you didn't go in and check out the window again?"

"I'm sure, I was going to look at it after breakfast."

"Well, I'm going to be up front this time. I shut it last night and this morning it's open."

"You're sure you closed it?" asked Grandpa, with furrowed brow.

"Yes."

They were both silent for a few minutes, then looked at each other. She could see he was as disheartened as she was. "Maybe we do have a ghost since Calvin, Jerry and Dillon, are all gone," she finally said.

"What do you mean Dillon's gone?"

"It's nothing I want to talk about right now, but I think I said and did some things that he can't forgive. All I can say is I'm sorry; I've done a lot of stupid things this year."

"And you told him you were sorry?"

"I didn't get the chance. Probably never will get a chance now."

"Oh, well, things will be better tomorrow. Lift that chin."

"Yeah, right. I'll take some coffee."

"You look like you're dressed for hard work. What do you have in mind today?" he asked.

"The Great Wallpaper Pull. I'm on my way over to rent a steamer now."

"Well, that sounds like quite the project. I'm doing some yard work, but I'll help you when I'm done."

"Thanks for the offer, but I don't want you to overdo. I'm pretty happy just knowing I have someone to do a little yard work around here." She kissed him on the forehead as she left. "I love you, Grandpa."

TAYLOR HAD TO DRIVE TO BOISE TO RENT A STEAMER. WHEN SHE finally arrived home, Dillon sat on the back steps watching Grandpa cut the grass. Pup chased Grandpa as if cutting the grass was just a big game.

Dillon stood when she stepped out of the car.

"Hello, Taylor." He didn't look much happier about being here than he did leaving the night before.

"Hello, Dillon."

Grandpa stopped the mower and approached them at the side of the car.

"Gilby called and said you wanted to talk to me."

Grandpa looked like the cat that swallowed the proverbial canary. No wonder she stretched the truth so much, it was genetic. If she gave him away then she would once again affirm how loony they were, and that would do more harm than good.

"I don't want your money," she said firmly.

"I'll take some," said Grandpa.

Dillon looked from Taylor to Gilby, then laughed.

It wasn't the least bit funny to her. "I have a job."

Gilby held up a finger. "Teachers are wealthy, you know. If not of monetary value think of the riches of helping a young person learn."

"Grandpa!"

Dillon laughed again.

"Grandpa, I don't think you're helping," she said frustrated.

"Actually, he is," Dillon said and laughed again. "Gilby, would you excuse us? I need to talk to Taylor."

They sat at the kitchen table, and she rubbed her nervous, sweating hands together. Dillon spoke first. "You know honesty is very important in a relationship."

She nodded, then said, "First, I want to apologize for looking at your computer. That was wrong. I promise to be direct from now on. Now, okay, let's get some things straight. Let's start at the beginning. Why did you help us? Was it out of guilt for selling us this property?"

"No...business is business."

"Then you didn't really have any guilty feelings, you know, to make you think you should stay around and help us?"

"Not really, no."

"Then why did you help us?"

"At first, I was a little concerned about you guys making it because I carry the contract on the house, but I knew I had enough assets, I wouldn't go broke.

"Actually, it all started when I drove by and saw you sitting on the front steps with your face in your hands. And being a little familiar with your situation, I stopped in to see what the problem was. But when you stood up and I saw you in that teacher outfit, that blue jumper with the apples on the pockets, I thought you were everything I ever dreamed about. I had to stick around and see if you were for real."

Misty-eyed now, she said, "Really?"

He nodded.

"Then why didn't you just ask me out?"

"Think back. I was the enemy remember. The only way to get to you was by way of the roof, or through Gilby."

"You put the roof on to get to know me better?" she asked incredulously.

"Yeah, but you just thought I was some poor gigolo."

"I thought you were a carpenter fixing my roof."

"You said something about gigolo, I know," he said with a smile.

"That's because of that older woman I saw you with."

"You know we were doing real good communicating for what, five minutes now? What older woman? I haven't dated any older women."

She knew that wasn't true and it bothered her, she almost changed the subject then decided on honesty all the way around. "I saw you with her, Dillon."

His jaw clenched. "And where were we?"

"At the falls that day. Remember when I had King with me? Do you want a description of her?"

"Oh, yeah." He started to chuckle, then threw back his head and laughed. "Oh. I guess you don't see the humor."

"No."

"That was my mother, KC. She came up to visit me."

Taylor crossed her arms and looked at him in stony silence.

"My mother will be thrilled to hear this." He chuckled again, gleefully, then leaned forward. "Taylor, you will never have to be jealous for the rest of your life, because there's no one like you. My mother is, let's see, forty-six. I was born when she was sixteen years old. She says we grew up together."

Feeling humbled, her lips formed an o. After a moment, she said, "It's not all just me. I was attracted to you when I thought you were a struggling carpenter. So why do you think I was only inter-ested in your money?"

"Good point."

"You're darn right. And I paid your bill just like anyone else."

"Yeah, that was a test."

She couldn't believe her ears. "A test?" she said with a hand on her chest.

"Don't get all huffy. You passed the test." He made eye contact. "I have my needs and wants, too. All along I've needed to see how or what you expect of me. Like whether you want a free ride or not. I come with baggage. Remember, I told you about Liz, the woman who wanted to marry me but not raise our kids?"

She nodded.

"I broke up with her shortly after she'd admitted the fact. To save face as well as keep the things I'd provided, she got a restraining order on me. Before I found out about it, I went to the apartment to get some things and she had me arrested."

That would explain the criminal record. This time she leaned forward. "I see now why you've been watching me. It's understandable. But I've told you all along, all I've ever wanted from you was your body," she said and winked.

They both turned to watch Pup and Gilby come in the back door. "Darn young kids expect the old man to take care of all the work around here. Is it safe to come in?"

Dillon stood up. "Sure Gilby. I've got a present for the two of you. It's in the truck, I'll go get it."

When he came back inside Dillon held a box. "Sit down, Gilby, and look." He pulled the top off the box and inside was a plaque with the name ADAM'S FAMILY inscribed upon it.

"Oh, I see you did make it down to the county office after all," Taylor said, then after a moment started laughing.

Gilby turned the box so he too could read the inscription. He also laughed. "Wouldn't you know it? Wouldn't you know it? Hey, you're not playing a joke on us now, are you?"

He smiled. "No. The original family had the name of Adams and a couple that died here before Shirley Wilson were descendants. So, it was kept in the family for quite some time."

"Well, at least it's not spelled A-d-d-a-m-s." Then she snapped her fingers and sang, "The Addams Family."

"Okay, do you want to hang this or not?" Dillon asked.

"I'm for it. They were the original family, and you have to have a sense of humor. What do you think, Grandpa?"

"Oh, I agree. Pup and I'll go hang it."

Dillon touched Taylor's hand. "Let's go up to the tower room."

"Yeah, I'm afraid there's something I need to tell you about it." However, she nearly forgot what she'd planned to say when he closed the door behind them and kissed her long and hard.

"Dillon, I've got to tell you something," she said against his lips and pulled back. "Last night I shut the door and this morning it was open. I think it happened at least one other time, too."

He frowned and looked behind her toward the door. "You sure?"

"No, I'm not trying to get you to move in with me. The next man who lives here has to marry me."

He chuckled and kissed her on the forehead. "Maybe I should check the door and see if it's actually catching when it shuts. Could be something as simple as that."

"Or, we've got a ghost."

Putting his arms around her, he tried to kiss her again, but she broke the hold. "I think we need to talk some more." She believed all this smooching had to stop if there wasn't any future in it.

Grudgingly he said, "Okay."

"I need to know. Am I what you need?"

"It's taken me a long time to find out. First, I thought you were whacko, then I thought you were a schemer, then I thought you were whacko again. And that was just today."

No doubt it was probably true, she decided, and softly chuckled.

"Well, you can be kind of hardheaded, but I think that you learn from your mistakes."

"And I've made a lot of them this year," she agreed.

He tried to kiss her again and she lifted her hand up between them. With a disarming smile he was able to back her up against the door, then he said, "You don't need to be taken care of, you're independent in your own right, even though you've had to budget like a miser to make ends meet around here. You have a career dream that you've followed through with. I respect all that in a woman. And you're sexy as hell."

He was about to pin her up against the door, but she hugged him instead. "You don't know how good that makes me feel, Dillon, because for a time I thought you weren't interested in me sexually."

"We haven't been ready for that. Believe me, I took lots of cold showers."

She backed away from the door because it hurt the back of her head and led him toward the window.

"And what about me? Am I what you need?"

"Why sure, you're rich," she said, glad when he laughed. His laugh proved to her that it wasn't going to be an issue anymore. There were many things she liked about Dillon, but before she could put them to words Dillon went down on one knee.

He sighed. "I guess our hearts have needed restoring as well as this old house."

They both nodded.

"Will you marry me, Taylor?"

She immediately checked his face for any signs of humor. Satisfied, she grew misty-eyed at his humble and hopeful face.

The door flew open, and Pup sauntered in waging his tail. Pup jumped up on Dillon and she blurted out, "Yes!"

"I think I found the answer to your ghost, Taylor," said Dillon, then took Pup out into the hall and shut the door. "Call him!"

"Pup! Come, Pup!"

The door flew open, and Dillon laughed. "It's Pup all right.

Since this door has a handle and not a knob, he jumps up and pushes the handle down and in he comes. What a smart dog!" He patted his head.

Taylor laughed, too. "I've got a name for him now."

"What is it?"

"Casper."

"Perfect."

EPILOGUE

Casper barked, wagged his tail, then sat and whined at the backdoor.

Taylor sat at the kitchen table flipping through a bride's magazine when Grandpa returned home from his first senior road trip.

"How was it, Grandpa?" she asked with a bright smile.

"Oh, wonderful. These trips are worth growing old for. Next time I'm going to take a trip down the Columbia Gorge and take in the off the road places."

"Sounds great. I'm happy for you."

"Dillon back from California, yet?"

"Tomorrow. Did I tell you he's going to try and get Jeff to relocate up here?"

"No, but Jeff shouldn't be surprised. He'll have at least had time to think about it." He stood behind Taylor, kissed the top of her head, and looked over her shoulder. He pointed at a featured wedding dress. "Nice. You still going through with it, huh?" he asked lightheartedly.

"You mean the marriage? Sure. I still can't believe everything's coming together so well."

"And when is this blessed event going to take place?"

"We decided to pick a day a week or two before school starts."

He took a seat beside her and rubbed Casper's head and neck. "Now are you both sure you want me to stay here? I would understand if you would want your privacy."

"We don't want you to move. This is going to be the house that we re-build. Besides that, there's enough room in this big old house for all of us to get lost. So, forget it."

"I have something to show you." He took the Trillium Falls newspaper from the table by the backdoor and set it before her.

"Oh, my goodness! You got your story published, and it's on the front page!"

"Well, I'm not letting the honor go to my head, since this is only a small-town newspaper, you know. Besides, who could resist a good ghost story?"

Grandpa decided to write a story telling all that had happened with the house, from the beginning of Calvin's stay until now, including the announcement of the engagement. His opinion was that the town needed to learn the history of the house, convinced that once they did the haunted house theory would finally vanish. She had to agree after she read the story.

"Did they edit anything?"

"No, not a thing."

Taylor laid the paper down and looked up at her grandfather. "Isn't it great to finally get through all this? And with our lives and health?"

"Yes it is, Granddaughter. I'm very glad you bought this house."

ABOUT THE AUTHOR

MARY VINE is an author, publisher, speaker and retired educator. She writes contemporary and historical romantic fiction, a time travel series, and inspirational children's books. Mary, and her husband can usually be found in Southwest Idaho or Northeast Oregon.

To learn more about Mary and all her books, visit her website http://authormaryvine.blogspot.com/

ALSO BY MARY VINE

CONTEMPORARY ROMANCE

Maya's Gold

A Place to Land

Secrets of Trillium Falls

Snake River Rendezvous

HISTORICAL ROMANCE

Wanting Moore

TIME TRAVEL SERIES

Nugget of Time

Goldbrick

Summer Solstice

INSPIRATIONAL CHILDREN'S BOOKS

The Big Guy Upstairs

Biju Silver Lining

Dragon Gilby

Dragon Gilby and Jamie Deer

www.ingramcontent.com/pod-product-compliance
Lightning Source LLC
Chambersburg PA
CBHW032039240626
47154CB00003B/995